# BY DANIEL CULL

# Planet of Fear

## Acknowledgements

Rachael and the boys for their constant love, support and inspiration.

Ray for always being available with notes, thoughts and comments and for constantly keeping me on the narrative straight and narrow.

Andy for his thoughtful guidance and assistance.

# 1

The floor shook and the walls burned with intense, radiating heat. James ran, forcing himself through the throng of people heading in the opposite direction. They were running for their lives, but he knew there was no point. Where could they possibly go?

He got to the command centre and looked at the few desperate souls who remained. They were pushing buttons and throwing switches but stopped what they were doing and turned to him, their eyes filled with relief and hope.

Aware that time was running out, James turned to address his staff, his body framed by the burning sky, which was visible through the window behind him.

"I'm sorry. You trusted me and I let you down. You followed my dream and now that dream will be the end for all of us. Thank you for your hard work; I know the people at home will remember you fondly."

He had never been good with words, and he knew that what he had said was deeply unsatisfactory, but there was no time for anything better. The disappointment in the room was palpable.

The ground beneath their feet shook again, and some debris from the ceiling tumbled down. James's assistant Connor, a young, red-haired engineer, spoke up.

"There must be something we can do."

"Vent the secondary air processor," James replied simply.

Connor looked at the screen before him, "but if we do that, the machine will explode."

James sighed sadly. "It's going to explode anyway, but if you vent the processor, it will happen six minutes later."

"What's the point? What can we do in that time?"

"You can change the world in six minutes. Use it anyway you would like."

The sky rumbled as air poured out of the processor into the atmosphere. James sat down at his console and started typing. The room fell silent as everyone began to type or record the last words they would ever say to the people they loved.

Six minutes later, far away from Earth, and unnoticeable in the night sky, a planet died.

Lucas ran, panting as he sped past the heaps of rubbish that lined the crumbling road. School had overrun. He was late and had little time.

He looked at the mess of twisted metal and broken glass and made a swift calculation, guessing he could save around two minutes and fifteen seconds. Taking the shortcut could be risky, however. He knew the rubbish heap well and it was a route his friends had often taken, gently mocking him as he trudged along the road to meet them on the other side. On the other hand, he could easily impale himself on a jagged piece of metal. With time running out, he decided it was worth the risk. Changing course, he launched himself at the pile. At first, he skipped easily over the refuse, following the path that his friends had made. An old trash bot suddenly shifted, however, and he lost his footing. He managed to regain it, but found himself lurching towards a torn, rusted solar shield. He spun around and slipped again. Thankfully, this time he was near the road on the other side and allowed his momentum to carry him forward and over the last few pieces of rubbish. He rolled to a stop, covered in dust. Lesson learned: he wouldn't be doing that again. He stood up, wheezing. Exercise outside was never a good idea. Without the benefit of the air re-processors that were built into most homes, deep breaths quickly filled the lungs with thick black pollutants. Lucas wasn't exactly athletic and knew there was a good chance he would later wake up retching.

It was a fairly quiet night, except for the usual angry shouting that accompanied the food demonstrations in the city half a kilometre away. He got to the accommodation block and looked up at the imposing concrete structure. His mum had said there were houses here once, with little gardens, sheds and garages. The growing population, the loss of much of the south and east of England to the sea and the increased need for farmland had led to the houses being demolished to make way for something that could contain more people. Lucas couldn't miss something he'd never known; to him this had always been home. It was certainly crowded, but the persistent murmur of a thousand conversations and the smell of a hundred meals comforted him.

Above the building, Lucas could already see the grimy grey sky beginning to clear. Tonight was the first time in 18 months that the sky would be free enough of pollution for stars to be visible, including his dad's. He'd already set the telescope up on the roof. He stumbled clumsily up the stairs, past the efficiently stacked living pods, quickly greeting neighbours that he knew almost as well as his own family. Finally, he was home. He excitedly threw open the door.

"Come on, Mum," he gasped, "it's nearly time."

His mother turned to look at him. He could just make out the Earth Science Division logo at the top of the message on the tablet in his mother's hand. Her eyes were red from crying. Lucas felt his heart sink. It didn't take a genius to know what was wrong. He knew in that moment he would never see his father again.

Days, months and years passed. The pain faded but did not go away. It helped that Lucas's mother was happy to talk about his father and their work together. After a while, though, she would go quiet and drift away from the conversation, her eyes in another place and time.

Eventually she went back to work and life was almost normal, until that night a few months later.

Lucas was lying in bed listening. He could never relax until he heard the reassuring sound of the front door closing after his mother got home. She would walk past his room to her own, and once he had heard the light switch flick off he would fall asleep. Tonight she got to Lucas's room and stopped, before gingerly opening the door.

She spoke quietly. "Lucas, are you awake?

Lucas turned on the lamp next to his bed. "Yeah, I'm awake, Mum. What's up?"

"You know I told you about the little houses with gardens?"

Lucas wasn't sure where this was going. "Yeah, Mum, I remember."

"I want that for you. Not just for you, for everyone, and I think they can do it, but not without me. I have to help them continue your dad's work so that people have the chance of a better life. In fact, a chance of surviving at all."

"But that's how dad..." Lucas stammered, he could never say the word "died", it was too real, too final, so he just left the sentence hanging in the air.

She held Lucas's hand comfortingly. "I know. But we've learned so much since then. We know what went wrong and it won't happen again. It means going a long way away, though, farther than anyone has ever been. I'm not going without you, so it's your decision: will you come?"

Lucas looked out of the window at the murky sky. Somewhere beyond the thick pollution, beyond the moon and beyond their solar system, a planet was waiting for him. He could almost see it there. It was calling to him, but it wasn't inviting; it was taunting him, telling him not to come and that terrible things would happen if he did. He looked at his mother, who was patiently waiting for an answer, and opened his mouth to respond.

# 2

Lucas looked out of the spacecraft's tiny window and saw the planet approaching rapidly. It was mostly a patchy red colour but, somewhere around the middle, there was a swirling cloud of blue and white, like a tornado made of cloud and sky. Proxima Centauri, the star around which Anora orbited, could just be seen, as it began to illuminate the planet's surface. Some people would have said it was a beautiful sight. Lucas was not one of them.

He remembered the months following his mother's question. After saying yes, he'd learned everything he could about the planet: the star it orbited, space travel, the terrain – anything that seemed relevant. He hoped these things would make him brave, excited even. It hadn't worked. His mother wouldn't believe him if he told her, he thought it pretty ridiculous himself, but he knew the planet had been speaking to him for months: teasing him, filling him with fear. Now he could actually see Anora. It was huge and getting bigger as they approached. Lucas felt like it was toying with him, inviting him closer only to attack him once he got there, like a monster in a movie.

He wriggled in the harness that pinned him to his seat. He had been uncomfortable ever since waking from cryo-sleep to prepare for arrival. Faster-than-light drives allowed travel over great distances by bending space. This meant that it only took months to travel to Earth's nearest star. For the drives to work, however, the ships had to be small, with little room for food, drink and entertainment. For that reason, Lucas and the other passengers had spent most of the journey in capsules that were filled with thick liquid and stacked high like cargo.

Getting into the capsule had been a little like entering a warm bath. The warmth had not lasted long, as the liquid was then suddenly frozen. As Lucas slept in the frozen fluid, his life had slowed to a crawl. He had no need for food or water and his heart barely beat. By the time he got out of the cryo-chamber he was fourteen years old, having passed his thirteenth birthday. While his friends on Earth would have grown during that time, he looked exactly as he had when his journey began.

Lucas had been told there would be no dreams during cryo-sleep, but he was sure he'd had some; he just couldn't remember what they were about. Possibly about the planet, which still dominated his thoughts. Or maybe he had dreamed about his father. He certainly felt his father's presence surrounding him. Whatever he had dreamt, he was sure it had been a nightmare, because of the familiar unsettled feeling deep in his stomach. Nowadays all he had were nightmares.

The fingernails on Lucas's clenched fists dug into his skin as they approached their destination. His mother, seated next to him and seeing his distress, smiled warmly. She looked calm and comfortable, as if she were in her armchair in their pod at home. That armchair seemed a very long way away now. She placed her hand on Lucas's, trying to steady it. She thought he was trembling because he was afraid of space travel, or nervous about what their new life would be like. That was part of it, but the main thing that scared Lucas was the closer they got to Anora, the louder the voice of the planet became.

Lucas felt rockets fire, slowing the ship as it neared the planet. He could feel the spacecraft heat up, as it penetrated Anora's limited atmosphere. Soon they were racing along, the stony, dusty ground hurtling by beneath them. In the distance, Lucas could see Nova Station: the base that would be his home for the next few years. It was a functional structure, with several domed habitats surrounding a much larger central building. Some distance behind that building stood the Terraformer, the cause of the storm that could be seen from space. It looked like a colossal chimney reaching to the heavens. It was impressive this close, shooting what looked like blue fire into the sky. In reality, it was a mix of nutrients, water and oxygen designed to bring life to this dead world.

Communication towers and solar panels surrounded the buildings, but otherwise there was little to see. Lucas knew that most of the station was beneath the planet's surface.

The machines had arrived before any people were sent to Anora. Automated vehicles, drills and diggers dropped by remotely piloted spacecraft. They had dug the tunnels that would become the foundation of Nova Station. The domes were parachuted down from the sky and clamped to the ground. The machines then laid cables between the solar panels and central buildings, bringing electricity to the planet. The first humans arrived once the basic structure of the base was in place; soldiers and military engineers trained to work in inhospitable conditions. They installed the Terraformer and put in computers, lights, kitchen equipment, beds, refrigeration units and everything else the base would need. Only now, several years after the Terraformer first became operational, were civilians like Lucas and his mother beginning to arrive.

The spacecraft slowed as it neared the base. Rotors slid out from canopies in the side of the craft and came spinning into life, pushing it higher into the sky, only for it to quickly drop down again, clicking into the docking tower on the side of the main habitation dome. The ship rocked as it settled into place. Lucas could hear clamps turning and locking, doors opening and the hiss of air as fresh oxygen entered the cabin. Another click told him that his harness was now released and could be removed. Despite his discomfort, he didn't take it off. His mother released her own harness and stood up, stretching. She reached down and removed Lucas's harness for him. He gripped the edge of his chair, fear clamping him in place more securely than any harness ever could. His mother put her hand gently on his arm.

"Come on, Lucas," she said excitedly, "let's take a look at our new home."

# 3

As they exited the ship, a tall, slightly overweight man greeted them. If his chubby form indicated his best years as a soldier were behind him, his perfectly pressed uniform, closely shaved face and neatly trimmed moustache did their best to tell a different story. The plasma rifle hanging over the man's shoulder pulsated with lethal power.

"Kane," the man said, offering his hand to Lucas's mother. "I'm in charge of this facility."

Lucas's mother took Kane's hand and shook it vigorously.

"Sarah Turner, and this is my son, Lucas. Do you have a first name, Mr Kane?"

Kane bristled at this. "It's Commander Kane. Rank is important while the base is still under military command."

"My apologies," Lucas's mother said. "Commander Kane, of course. I thought that all military personnel had returned to earth."

"Most of the official military contingent have indeed left, but I remain in command for now."

"I look forward to working with you on the transfer to civilian control," she said warmly.

Kane looked her up and down, as if assessing a new challenge. "Of course, Ms Turner, all at the appropriate time. For now, perhaps you'd like to see the rest of the base."

Lucas's mother turned to her son. "That would be wonderful, don't you think?"

Lucas, who had been staring at Kane's plasma rifle nervously, feigned as much enthusiasm as he could muster. "Yeah, Mum, brilliant, great, love to."

Lucas stopped before his fake enthusiasm became too much. His mother took his hand as they followed Kane out of the docking bay. She could always sense Lucas's insincerity and said to him quietly, "Thanks for giving this a go, I know how hard it is for you."

Cables ran along the tunnel walls, and bright, red LED lights lit the way. There were doors everywhere, leading to corridors and tunnels that stretched far into the distance. People were constantly coming and going. They were focused entirely on their tasks and didn't give Lucas or his mother a second glance. Kane stopped at a door and hit a switch that sent it sliding open with a soft hiss, revealing a group of youths around Lucas's age. Each wore a uniform much like Kane's. They stood next to benches, building and dismantling weaponry.

Kane addressed Lucas. "You will be taught with the Nova cadets here," he explained. "Although they're civilians, I have been working hard with them. I think you'll be impressed with their military knowledge."

"They've got guns," Lucas said incredulously.

"Just replicas. As per orders from Earth Command, this is the only weapon on the base." He indicated the plasma rifle. "Doesn't do any harm to give them some weapons training, though. What are your particular areas of expertise?"

Lucas looked nervously at the swift precision of the cadets. "I'm pretty good at English I guess, and maths. Bit more of a thinker than a fighter."

Kane was unimpressed. "We'll soon knock some military discipline into you. Survival skills, that's what you need on Anora."

Lucas's mother stepped in. "I hope that isn't all you've been teaching them, Commander. As the base moves under civilian control, we will expect the students to have a much wider range of knowledge: maths, history, science, literature..."

"If the base moves to civilian control, Ms Turner, you can teach any fluffy nonsense you like. Until then I will decide the subject matter."

"Commander, you'll be aware that Earth command expects a full curriculum to be taught to off-world pupils."

"But Earth command are not here, Ms Turner. I am. And I know that out there is an inhospitable planet of dust and rock, with death waiting around every corner. I'm equipping these cadets to survive."

Kane looked at Lucas's mother with a steely gaze that she easily, and unblinkingly, met. "Things are going to have to change then," she countered.

The silence that followed was thick with a tension that made Lucas feel uncomfortable. "You know what," he finally said. "I'd love to see the rest of the base now."

Lucas's mother smiled at this blatant lie and allowed Kane to be free from her stare.

"Of course," Kane mumbled, "let's continue."

They reached the end of the corridor and stepped through a door into the command centre. Computers lit up the room, with screens monitoring every aspect of the planet. There were graphs and charts measuring the temperature and panels displaying weather and atmospheric composition.

A man stepped forward from the bank of computers and offered his hand to Lucas's mother. "Hi there," he said, "Sarah Turner, I presume. I've been so excited to meet you. Nathan Pearson, I'm head of tech around here."

Lucas's mother surveyed the room. "There's certainly a lot of tech to be head of," she said. "This is my son, Lucas."

"Great to meet you guys. We've taken things as far as we can and we're going to need your expertise to continue to make progress." There was a deep rumble from the sky outside. "Looks like you got here just in time."

"Of course – the storms!" Lucas's mother said. "Do you get them every night?"

"Like clockwork," Pearson replied, "and they're getting more powerful.

"As the atmosphere develops, there will be stronger and more frequent storms until it settles," Lucas's mother added.

Pearson gestured towards the Terraformer, "And it's your amazing machine that's creating that atmosphere. Do you want to see it?"

Lucas's mother's excited face was all the confirmation Pearson needed. He gestured to one of the computer operators and instructed, "Open her up."

The roof of the dome opened slowly, revealing a transparent window. They had a perfect view of the Terraformer in all its glory.

Lucas's mother seemed lost in the beauty of it, hypnotised by the never-ending stream of blue fire. "It's *our* amazing machine, Mr Pearson. I designed it with my husband."

"Nathan, just Nathan," the man replied. "You and your husband certainly built something incredible. I was so sorry to hear about what happened to him."

"Yes, I'm aware of your husband's sacrifice to get us to this point," Kane interjected. "He was a great man."

This was how people usually talked about Lucas's father: as if he were some legendary figure who'd changed the universe. Lucas remembered his father as a real living person, however: mostly kind, occasionally angry and full of love. He recalled his father explaining the Terraformer to him, telling him how pollution and overpopulation meant that humans would need to find new homes in the stars. The Terraformer was vital in helping them do that. It could take a dry, dead planet and give it an atmosphere, water and weather. Over time, the planet would come to life. There would be rivers, grass, hills and trees. A home away from home. His father had sacrificed his life for that dream. Lucas didn't see his father as a hero, or his sacrifice as great and noble. He knew his father didn't want to die, that he would have given anything to be standing next to Lucas at that moment. Lucas missed his father and, as he looked at the Terraformer, he couldn't help but hate the machine that had taken him away.

# 4

That night, Lucas struggled to sleep. His bedroom was tiny, and he had been unable to bring much to make it feel like home. All he had was his father's medal - for services to Earth Science Division - and his computer tablet, which he used to read all he could about the planet, hoping that the information would help keep him alive.

He stared at the tablet, specifically at the unread message that was blinking in the corner. His finger hovered over it for a few seconds. No, he decided, not tonight. He placed the tablet next to the medal on his bedside table and tried to sleep.

In the accommodation block, he had been surrounded by noise, but he had found the constant murmur of conversation comforting. He had even gotten used to occasional raised voices or the thumping bass of an inconsiderate party. The noise here was different: cold, sterile and somehow haunting. The base was a 24-hour operation, with as many people working at night as in the daytime, so there was a constant throng of movement and discussion. Unlike the accommodation block, however, it wasn't the pleasant sound of friends or families chatting, but the sharp, clipped tones of orders being made and obeyed. He could also hear the automated machines digging deep underground. Outside his window, the storm continued to rage, pounding the dome with water and gale-force winds, while the sky glowed with the light of the Terraformer.

When Lucas did finally sleep, he saw his father in his dreams. The Terraformer was behind him but something was wrong. He was trying to run as the blue fire began to spill out of cracks appearing in the body of the machine. Suddenly, the world was awash with blue and his father was gone. Then the dream moved on. Lucas felt himself flying over the planet's surface, not in a spaceship this time, but feeling the dust and wind on his face. As he flew he could hear a noise. It was the voice of Anora, but it wasn't whispering to Lucas anymore, it was screaming. It was afraid of the Terraformer, of the atmosphere growing in the sky; it didn't want to change, it just wanted to be left alone. The planet itself began to crack, the blue fire forcing it apart. The scream was getting louder, almost intolerably so. It was then that Lucas's mother woke him.

"Come on," she said eagerly, "it's time to go out onto the surface."

After a filling, nourishing and taste-free breakfast, Lucas found himself standing in a massive hangar. It contained four enormous vehicles; three were locked in their charging units, and the other was being prepared for their trip. It seemed to be more wheel than anything else, with gigantic rubber tyres, taller than Lucas, leading to a comparatively small driving area on top. Pearson introduced Lucas and his mother to it.

"The Planetary Exploration Vehicle, PEV for short, is designed for traversing extremely hostile terrain. That's why it has a powerful suspension system and these large, solid rubber tyres." He hit the tyres hard with a spanner. "The Terraformer has been at work for over two years, so the atmosphere is breathable but very thin, like being on the top of a mountain. Although you would be able to survive out there for a while, you would eventually lose consciousness. For this reason, although there's no need to wear a full spacesuit, you will need this.

He handed Lucas a device with a mouthpiece in the middle and two small canisters on either side, giving another to Lucas's mother. "This is a breather. It contains extremely compressed $CO_2$ and will allow you to breathe normally on the surface for up to eight hours. Don't lose it."

Lucas gripped the precious contraption.

"So, are you ready to go?" Pearson asked.

The enormous doors began to slowly open, revealing the rocky surface of the planet outside. Lucas looked at his mother's excited face and the ominous, unknown terrain. Of course he wasn't, but he smiled at his mother and climbed up the ladder to the cab of the vehicle.

Soon they were bouncing over the surface of the planet. Lucas consoled himself that at least they were moving away from the Terraformer. They drove past the habitation domes and the communication towers. Pearson knew the surface well and skilfully navigated past craters and boulders, Anora's rocky mountains casting huge shadows over the PEV. He turned to Lucas, shouting over the mighty rumble of the engine. "What do you think? Beautiful, isn't it?"

Lucas stared at the landscape. He hadn't seen anything like it before. It was vast, empty and somewhat terrifying. Words tumbled out of his mouth. "It's certainly big, but it's sort of bleak and dusty." He was aware Pearson was looking confused. "But beautiful, yeah, you know, kind of."

Lucas suddenly noticed how quickly the rocks and mountains were moving past. "Are you sure you should be driving this fast, Mr Pearson?" he asked.

"Call me Nathan, and we're actually only going about 15 kilometres per hour, it just seems faster because of the rough ground. Don't worry, I know this planet like the back of my hand."

Lucas's mother put her arm around Lucas. "Sorry Nathan, my son's just nervous."

"Perfectly understandable, plenty of ways to die out here. We should be heading back now anyway. I don't want to go too far from the base on your first trip out."

Suddenly, Lucas spotted something. "Hey, what's that?"

Just ahead of them was a fenced-off area. Signs surrounded it that said: "Keep Out", "Danger" and "Heavily Toxic Environment."

The PEV slowed as it approached.

"I've got no idea," Pearson admitted.

"It's nothing to be worried about," Lucas's mother said, "It's just an experiment, but it's still dangerous, so best to keep away."

"But what is it?" Lucas insisted.

His mother chose to ignore the question and addressed Pearson instead. "Let's turn around and head back."

Lucas looked past the mesh fence. He could see a large, dark lake gently bubbling. People were walking around it, testing the liquid and adjusting strange devices.

Lucas was confused. What was this place and why was it so far from the main base? What made it so dangerous and what did his mother know about it? As he considered these questions, one of the workers walked over to a large switch and threw it. A burst of powerful electricity shot through the lake.

The lake looked alive now, churning and swirling. Lucas kept staring at the bubbling liquid as the PEV turned to head back to the base. The bubbles were hypnotic. He could almost hear them whispering to him, adding to the dark, haunted voice of the planet. Why wouldn't his mother tell him what was going on? He felt confused and unsettled. One thing was certain, however: he didn't want to be anywhere near this dark lake again.

# 5

It was Lucas's mother's first day at work, but before she went to analyse the performance of the Terraformer and, presumably, check on the experiment at "the lake", she walked Lucas to his first class.

As they reached the classroom, she tidied up his hair and said what she always said: "Just be yourself."

Lucas took a moment to absorb this useless piece of advice and smiled at his mother. "I'll be fine," he said.

Kane was teaching, and as he entered, Lucas noticed the frosty look that passed between Kane and his mother.

Once his mother had left, Lucas looked around for somewhere to sit. Before he could find anywhere, Kane addressed the class loudly and firmly, "Stand to attention."

The students leapt up from their desks and, seemingly in one effortless movement, stood bolt upright behind them.

"We have a new pupil with us today, just arrived from Earth. Lucas Turner."

As Kane met Lucas's eyes, he said to the class, "I want you to help him adjust to life here on the base." There was something in the way he said it, however, that made it seem like a threat. Kane

27

turned back to the class, "We'll soon make him into a survivor."

Then he addressed Lucas directly. "So, son, what would you need to do to survive in hostile territory?"

Lucas stumbled for an answer. "Maybe find a takeaway or something."

Someone tittered, Kane looked annoyed.

"Sorry," Lucas said. "Food, I'd look for food."

Kane waited for a moment and then, realising that this was all he was going to get, barked suddenly to the class, "How do we survive in hostile territory?"

The class barked back, loudly and perfectly in unison, "Be prepared, know the territory, seek shelter."

A girl at the front of the class looked at Lucas and laughed to herself, clearly unimpressed by his pathetic answer. She had dark brown hair and eyes and looked strong and confident in a way that made Lucas envious. The girl frowned at him and Lucas realised he was staring. He nervously looked down at his feet.

"Very good," Kane said. He assessed Lucas for a moment. "I think we'll start with some basic combat training."

The other cadets pushed the desks and chairs to the side of the room, clearing a space in the middle. They formed a circle.

"Right, Williams, Peterson, you show him how it's done."

Two boys stood forward and began to circle each other, looking intently for an opening or a weakness. Suddenly, Williams struck, firing a punch at Peterson's head. Peterson dodged the punch and countered with a blow to Williams's side. This clearly caused Williams some pain and he jumped back. The two boys circled each other again. Peterson struck first this time, aiming a kick at Williams's thigh. Williams was prepared for this and he grabbed Peterson's leg with lightning speed, twisting it around. With Peterson off balance, it was easy for the other boy to throw him to the floor and pin him there.

Kane seemed satisfied. "Very good, boys, very good." He looked at Lucas, "time for you to give it a go."

Lucas, who had never thrown a punch in his life, tried to politely decline. "I'm not sure this is really for me. I'm more on the academic side.

Kane dismissed Lucas's protests out of hand. "Nonsense," he said. "It'll help make a man out of you."

He pointed to the girl in the circle who had laughed at Lucas. "Becky, show him what you can do." He briefly assessed Lucas again before adding, "better go easy on him."

The girl stepped out of the circle, as did Lucas, somewhat reluctantly. Lucas addressed her quietly when they met in the middle, "Why Becky?"

"I'm sorry?" she replied.

"Commander Kane calls everyone by their surname, but he called you Becky."

"Oh, that's just because he's my dad."

The information did not make the impending fight any more appetising, and Lucas sighed. "Of course, he would be; it's been that kind of day."

Despite herself, Becky laughed at Lucas's sarcasm.

"Right, let's see what you can do," Kane declared.

Assuming this meant the fight was going to start, Lucas stood back from Becky and made fists with his hands, putting them up somewhere in front of his face in an attempt to imitate the actors he'd seen fighting in movies.

Becky looked almost sorry for him as she hit him with a blow to his side. Unfortunately, because Lucas's hands were still in front of his face, it connected cleanly. Lucas arched at the pain, lowering his hands. Becky took the opportunity to punch him in the head. Although she was not hitting him as hard as she could, the punch still hurt. Lucas stumbled back and swung at Becky with one of his fists. Becky didn't even need to dodge the punch as it whipped through the air some distance in front of her face. This left Lucas open and gave her the opportunity to catch his arm and use it to pin him to the floor. Lucas was relieved it was over.

Kane didn't look happy. "I thought you'd be bad, but I never imagined you'd be that useless."

"Maybe I'm not cut out for combat," Lucas mumbled from his position on the floor.

"Nonsense, we just need to get back to basics. Bring me CARL."

In response to the commander's request, a robot, about Lucas's height, trundled into the room on tank-like wheels. There was nothing that looked like a head, just six metallic arms hanging from a large torso.

"This is CARL," the Commander explained. "It stands for Combat Assimilating Robotic Lifeform. We use it to start gently guiding cadets through basic combat techniques. Why don't you give it a try? CARL, training programme Alpha One, please."

The robot moved towards Lucas. One of its metallic arms jabbed towards his face. It was a slow, gentle jab, however, and Lucas easily avoided it. The robot threw one of its other arms, again gently enough that Lucas could easily dodge the other way.

Kane seemed pleased. "Good, now you're getting it. Let's try Alpha Two, CARL."

31

The robot spun into life more quickly now, using three of its arms to throw punches at Lucas. By moving around the room, Lucas was able to avoid the robot, but it was getting harder, and he was beginning to stumble.

Kane didn't seem to notice Lucas's difficulty and continued to encourage him. "That's it. You're finding that survival spirit. Can you feel the blood coursing through your veins?"

Lucas felt only tiredness as he continued to dodge and duck the advancing robot. "I think I'm done with R2-D2 now, Commander."

"Nonsense," Kane retorted. "We're just getting started. CARL, let's skip straight to Alpha Four."

Lucas spotted Becky's face in the crowd. She was clearly not convinced Alpha Four was a good idea. Lucas quickly saw why. The top half of the robot was now spinning and ducking around, the tracks on its base speeding up. It was using all its arms to swipe and jab at Lucas. One of them caught him and sent him tumbling to the ground. He quickly got up, only to be caught by another arm, which sent him over again. Lucas rolled away as the Robot's wheels sped past his head.

"Dad, he's had enough," Becky shouted.

"No, he hasn't," Kane shouted back. "We need to make a soldier out of him."

The robot attacked Lucas ferociously. Desperate, panicked and finding himself stuck in a corner, Lucas grabbed a chair and threw it at CARL. Sparks flew off the robot's body, but it kept coming. The impact of the chair seemed to have done more harm than good. One of the robot's arms was jerking erratically, while the others flailed quickly and randomly in all directions. The robot's torso was turning around and back with great speed and force, and its tracks were spinning faster and faster. The robot was malfunctioning. Lucas managed to roll out of the corner, but not before receiving a blow to his leg. Unable to stand, he looked imploringly at Kane.

Kane was giving him no sympathy. "Get up, boy, get up and fight. Survival of the fittest."

The robot was nearly upon Lucas now, its arms whirling towards his head. There was no way he could stop it, and as he watched the robot hurtle towards him, he knew he was going to die.

# 6

Suddenly, Becky ran from the watching circle of cadets and launched herself at CARL. The robot wasn't programmed to defend itself, only attack, so it had no interest in what Becky was doing. She still had to hang on, though. She used one arm and her legs to wrap herself tightly around the turning, lurching top half of the robot and managed to use her free arm to rip out the cables connecting the battery to its torso. It continued to flail around for a few seconds, groaned loudly and then slumped to a stop.

With the robot out of action, all eyes were now on Lucas, curled up on the floor. He was unmoving, apart from the gentle rise and fall of his chest. Realising the room was now silent, he looked up, the fear plainly visible on his face.

Kane was unhappy. "Becky, that was insubordination."

"But Dad, he was going to get hurt."

"Then let him. He needs to toughen up." Kane looked directly at Becky, "Leave. I'll deal with you later."

Becky stomped off, but instead of being cross with her father, she glared at Lucas as she left, annoyed that his pathetic display had put her in this position.

Kane looked at Lucas on the floor and showed no sympathy. "You see now what it takes? You can't survive here, you haven't got the right stuff. This isn't a place for civilians."

Lucas stood up and tried to gather as much dignity as he could, which was very little. He opened his mouth to tell Kane what he thought of him and his military discipline, to unleash his rage at being humiliated, but the words wouldn't come. Instead, he ran out of the room.

Lucas ran through doors and down corridors with no idea where he was heading. Soon he was lost in the maze of the base. He came upon a door that said "Observation Platform." He opened it, stepped through and saw a ladder leading up. He started climbing.

When he got to the top, he found himself at the tallest part of the base, with a view of the whole of Anora.

"Hey there," a voice said behind him. Lucas turned and saw Pearson, who was setting up a camera on the edge of the platform. "So, you found it then," Pearson added, "my little sanctuary. From here, you can almost see the whole planet. Not many people bother to come up here anymore though, they prefer to rely on the cameras to monitor things for them." He waved at the camera he had just installed and the many others bolted to the viewing platform. "But there's not much that compares to standing here and taking it all in for yourself. Our new home."

Lucas looked at the view in silence. What Pearson found inspiring, he found terrifying. Pearson noticed Lucas lost in silence and turned to him. "Is everything OK?"

"Yeah, everything's fine," Lucas replied unconvincingly.

"I'll let you stay here for a while to get your thoughts together. Just don't mess with my equipment, OK."

Pearson descended the ladder, leaving Lucas to survey his own, personal planet of fear.

When Lucas arrived back at his room that evening, it didn't take much cajoling for his mother to get the story out of him. When she found out what had happened in class, she was enraged.

"Just don't do anything over the top, Mum," Lucas implored.

"Don't worry, honey, I won't, but it's time Kane understood how things are going to work around here."

Kane and Lucas's mother contacted Earth the following day, from a small, private room. Although Lucas didn't hear what was said, voices were raised and Lucas saw Kane leave the chamber later that morning, his face full of rage and thunder. Kane caught Lucas's eye and Lucas could tell that behind

his dark, angry eyes was only one thought.
Revenge.

# 7

That night the storm raged as it had the night before. Again, Lucas dreamed fitfully of his father, the planet and his empty loneliness, four light-years from home. At some point during the night, his worries drove him awake. He reached for his tablet and stared at the unopened message again. He wanted to read it, but it scared him. These were the last words that his father had ever said to him. What if they didn't give the comfort and hope that he desperately needed? He turned the tablet off, put it down and focused on trying to get back to sleep.

The next day, Lucas was due to attend orientation class on the planet's surface. His mother assured him Kane had been spoken to and there wouldn't be a repeat of what had happened before.

"I just don't wanna go, Mum," Lucas implored. "Can't I just stay here?"

"You can't just hide away from people, no matter how unfair and cruel they may seem to be," she replied, giving Lucas what he assumed was meant to be a comforting smile. He did not smile back.

His mother continued. "You didn't deserve to lose your dad, and I know you miss your home, but this is where we are now, our new adventure, and we need to make the best of it. You'll find kindness out there, you'll make friends, but you have to be open to it, you have to meet people halfway."

Lucas knew how hard things had been for his mother since his father's death, and he hated adding to her problems. "OK, Mum, I'll do my best, I promise. I'll literally be the friendliest human on the planet."

Soon, he was standing on the planet's surface, wearing thick, heavy overalls, his breather in his hand and a heavy rucksack on his back. The Nova cadets stood in a line either side of him. He tried his best to mimic their stance, legs apart, hands behind his back. Kane arrived in a PEV and climbed down to address the cadets.

"Attention," he commanded.

Lucas again copied the others, standing as straight as he could with his hands by his side. Despite the events of the past two days, Kane did not pay any particular attention to Lucas. He paced up and down in front of the cadets. "Today, we will be spending time on the surface," he barked in his military style. "This is a new planet, with unknown dangers everywhere. You will find food, flares, a communicator, water, first aid, and insulation packs in your backpacks. All useful tools if you find yourself lost."

Lucas touched his backpack, comforted by its contents. He patted the side pocket where he had placed his father's medal. He was sure his most precious belonging would bring him luck.

Kane continued. "None of the items you carry will keep you alive, however, if you are afraid. Fear is your enemy; fear will stop you from thinking clearly; fear will make you react more slowly; fear will kill you. You are highly trained cadets, there is nothing that you should be afraid of. I will be following behind in the PEV and you'll be walking at a steady marching pace, which should allow everyone to keep up."

Kane climbed up the ladder to the PEV and shouted from the top, "March!"

The cadets moved off. Lucas found himself next to Becky. The pace was manageable, and, for the first time, he began to appreciate the beauty of the planet's surface, with the light from Proxima Centauri glistening off it. Every so often, he would glance at Becky and try to make eye contact, maybe start a conversation. Her eyes remained fixed firmly forward, however. She had no interest in talking to Lucas.

An hour later, the PEV was still bouncing along behind the cadets. The mood was a little more relaxed, and pockets of conversation had broken out. The sun was high in the sky, the beams bouncing off the mountains and shining through the random clouds of foggy atmosphere created by the Terraformer. It was incredible to see such an immense space, untouched by people. Lucas felt a closeness to this lonely place. For now, the voice of the planet was silent. Even without it, the untamed majesty around him made Lucas think that people should leave it alone and allow it to drift in space unpolluted. Then he remembered his promise to his mother. She wanted him to get out into the world and meet people halfway, and he'd said he would try. He glanced over at Becky again. There was no time like the present.

"Thank you for helping me yesterday," he ventured.

"I wouldn't have had to help you if you weren't so useless," she responded.

"I guess that's true," Lucas replied, somewhat deflated.

They continued to march, and Becky began to melt a little. "I'm sorry, it's just that you shouldn't be here, not yet anyway. It's dangerous. We're trained, and you're not. You don't know what you're doing, and you could get yourself killed."

"Believe me, it wasn't my choice. I don't want to be here any more than you want me to be here."

Becky smiled. "You'd be surprised how much I don't want you to be here."

"I think you'd be surprised how much I don't want to be here."

"Fair enough, we'll agree that we both really don't want you here."

"Happy with that."

It felt like the ice had been broken. As they marched, Lucas shared with Becky some of the things he'd learned about the planet from his reading. He told her about the mountains and craters - named after the people who'd discovered them - about the irregular orbit of the planet around Proxima Centauri and the Terraformer and how it worked. He didn't mention his father; it didn't seem like that kind of conversation. Becky wasn't a great talker, she was from a military family and had been taught to listen and obey rather than challenge or question, but she seemed content to listen as Lucas let his knowledge spill out. For the first time in a long time, he felt that he had made a friend.

The PEV pulled alongside the cadets, and the canopy slid open. "Halt," Kane shouted.

They came to an immediate stop and lined up, obediently awaiting instruction.

"You aren't going to learn survival skills with me following behind you, so you're now going to find your way back to base on your own. Williams and Peterson have digital maps of the terrain so you shouldn't get lost. Stay together, rely on each other and you'll be fine. Nightfall is in three hours, so if you're not back at base in two, we'll be out to find you. There are trackers in all your suits so that shouldn't be a problem, although I don't expect to have to use them. Rely on your training and remember: fear is your greatest enemy."

The canopy closed, and the PEV started making its way back to the base. The cadets marched on with Williams directing. Lucas did not feel sure about this at all. Were they ready to face this empty planet by themselves?

# 8

Lucas and the cadets continued to walk. Without the supportive sound of the PEV following behind, the conversation began to dry up, and they headed back towards the base mainly in silence. Lucas knew they were going broadly in the right direction, as the sun, which had been in front of them when they set off, had completed its path through the sky during their journey and was in front of them again. Some of the terrain looked different, however, and Lucas did not see the craters he had so eagerly described to Becky on the way out. They were taking a slightly different route on the journey back.

Then, a little way away, Lucas saw it: the experimental lake. The afternoon was drawing on, and the sunlight was beginning to fade, so the flashes of electricity through the lake could be seen as a harsh, intermittent glow, lightening the darkening sky. Lucas hoped no one else had seen it.

"What's that," Williams shouted, immediately dashing Lucas's hopes.

"I'm sure it's nothing,' Lucas said, "Probably best to keep heading back."

"What is it, though?" Williams continued. "I want to see what it is."

Peterson, always ready to agree with Williams, declared, "Me too."

Lucas did not want to go anywhere near the dark lake again. "It might not be safe, and it's getting late. You can always ask someone to take you out in the morning."

Becky seemed uncertain too. "Maybe he's right."

"What's the matter?" Williams countered. "Scared?"

This had the desired effect on Becky. "Fine, let's take a look. Better make it quick, though."

Lucas unhappily followed behind as the cadets headed for the lake.

It took another twenty minutes to get there, and the sun continued to head towards the horizon. Once there, the group hid in a crater as they watched the staff finish for the day and leave in two PEVs. Lucas saw his mother among them.

The site now empty, the cadets headed up to the lake and circled the fence surrounding it, trying to catch a glimpse of whatever it was hiding. Lucas was keen to get away as soon as possible. "We've seen it now," he said. "Let's head back."

Williams shook the gate that barred his way. "But I still don't know what it is," he protested. He started exploring the fence, looking for weaknesses. "I want to get in there."

Becky spoke up. "They're going to be annoyed if they have to come out and get us. Let's go."

"I thought daddy said fear was bad," Peterson taunted. "You afraid like your new little best friend?"

"He's not my friend," Becky countered, ignoring the hurt expression on Lucas's face. "You want to get in so badly, then get out of my way."

She slipped some laser cutters out of her backpack and cut a small hole in the fence, large enough for one person to wriggle through. She pulled the fencing away and beckoned to Williams.

Now there was no barrier to getting to the lake, Williams looked unsure. He didn't dare say anything, so instead laughed with affected confidence and slipped through the hole. The other cadets did the same, leaving only Lucas and Becky.

"I'm not sure this is a good idea," Lucas said nervously.

"You could always stay out here by yourself," Becky replied.

Lucas looked at the shadowy wasteland, weighed up his options and pushed himself through after the others. Becky was close behind.

Whatever the lake was filled with wasn't water: it was something thick and black. The dark pool had an immediate impact on the cadets and they stared at it in haunted silence.

As was often the case, Williams was the first to speak, breaking the spell by saying, "It's just a sewage dump or something."

"You should jump in then; you'd be right at home," Peterson said, laughing and grabbing Williams, pretending to push him in.

"No!" Lucas cried out. "Get away. It isn't safe."

"What's the matter, coward?" Williams taunted. "You don't like the poo lake? Is there anything on this planet you're not afraid of?"

"Just get away from the edge."

Williams started leaning towards the pool. "You afraid I'm going to fall in?"

"It's not safe."

Now Peterson was messing around near the edge too. "Not everything's safe, wimp." He arched his back as if tumbling backwards. "Maybe I'm going to fall in?"

Williams leant closer. "Or maybe it'll be me."

The events that followed happened so quickly that it was hard to recount them afterwards. Williams leant too close to the edge and began to slip. He instinctively grabbed Peterson to pull himself back up, but this pulled Peterson off balance, and he teetered towards the lake. Lucas had been watching the pair intently, terrified of what might happen. Seeing Peterson falling, he leapt forward and pushed him clear. Unfortunately, there was no one to grab Lucas, and his momentum took him over. He collided with the black liquid and flailed around for a moment. He was a reasonable swimmer, but he continued to sink no matter what he did as if the thick fluid were pulling him down. The last thing he saw was the cadets shouting and yelling, with Becky trying to reach out to him. Then the ooze closed over him, and he was gone.

# 9

Panic seized hold of the cadets, who continued to call for Lucas.

"We've got to go in after him," someone said.

"You saw what happened. It pulled him under. They'd drown too," countered someone else.

Becky kept shouting Lucas's name, but the lake's surface remained unbroken. "We've got to use the radio to get someone to help."

"He's been in there for at least five minutes," Williams replied with unsettling calmness. "He's gone, and he's not coming back."

"No," Becky pleaded. "We've got to do something."

Peterson spoke up. "What we've got to do is leave. We're not supposed to be here. If someone finds us, we're in big trouble. The runt's gone. We've got to take care of ourselves."

Becky took a long look at the still surface of the lake. "No, there's got to be something."

Williams took charge. "You can stay here and stare at that lake if you want, but the rest of us are leaving, and, if anyone asks, we were never here."

Williams pulled himself back through the hole in the fence, and, one by one, the cadets snaked through after him. Soon Becky was alone, still desperately hoping for some sign of life from the lake. It remained stubbornly unmoving. Aware that the cadets were heading away and realising that there was nothing to be gained in waiting for Lucas when his re-emergence was impossible, she followed the others.

As the group made their way back to the base, the evening storm started brewing in the sky behind them. They walked for an hour as it grew in intensity. The mood was sombre, their guilt suppressing any chance of conversation. Before long, they saw the PEV, headlights blazing, leaping over the terrain towards them. The canopy opened as it got to them, and Kane shouted out, "Attention, Nova cadets."

The cadets lined up in front of the PEV, and Kane climbed down. He strode up and down the line angrily. The teenagers stood in silence, heads bowed. "I expected better from you. You could have been caught in the storm. You were trained for this, and you let me down."

As he walked up the line for the third time, he came to a sudden realisation and did a quick count. "Hold on, where's the wimp?"

More silence. None of the cadets wanted to be the first to speak. Finally, Williams broke the tension. "He's gone, sir."

"What do you mean, gone?"

"He got scared and ran off. We tried to find him. That's why we're late."

Kane looked horrified. The kid had annoyed him, but he didn't want him lost. He looked to the one cadet he knew he could trust. "Is this true, Becky?"

Becky paused. She could feel the other cadets' eyes burning into her. "Yes, Dad, it's true."

Kane looked at the advancing storm, "There isn't much time." He took a computer tablet from the cab and brought up a map of the planet. There was a flashing rectangle indicating the PEV and a group of dots surrounding it, giving the position of Kane and the cadets. There was nothing else. He brought up the list of everyone on the expedition; all were highlighted green except for Lucas. Instead, the name Lucas Turner flashed red next to the words "tracker offline".

"His tracker's not working," Kane confirmed. "Where did this happen?"

"About five kilometres back there," Peterson lied, pointing towards what was now the storm's centre.

Kane didn't want to leave someone to die, but he knew how dangerous a storm on the planet could be.

"Right, back to the base, double time."

The cadets marched at a quick pace, the PEV behind them lighting the way.

Soon they were at the hangar. The giant door slid open, revealing a large group of worried-looking parents who had gathered to wait for their children. As the cadets entered the base, their mums and dads ran up, hugging or putting blankets around them. Some of the teenagers cried, but many were silent, their emotions pinned inside them by what they'd done. Becky walked off alone.

Lucas's mother searched for her son in the crowd, her face relieved and smiling. As she moved past child after child, her expression changed as panic returned. When she saw Kane walk up to her, she knew something was wrong.

"Where's Lucas?"

"Something happened," Kane replied calmly. "He got scared. He ran away."

"No, no, he didn't. He wouldn't do that."

"You know what your son's like, Ms Turner. He's a sensitive, fearful boy."

"No, you're wrong. You don't know him like I do."

"He was never cut out for life on this planet. He put the rest of the group at risk."

"He wouldn't run away."

"I'm afraid he did."

"No, that's not what happened.

Lucas's mother started moving through the cadets, talking to each one. "Tell the truth, what happened? What happened to my son?"

None of them would make eye contact or speak. Their parents began to move them away from her intense questioning.

The rain was starting to hammer on the roof, and the wind howled outside. The doors shook with the power of the arriving storm.

Lucas's mother grabbed Kane's arm. "We've got to go out and find him."

"No one's going out in this weather. The boy's been out there on his own for hours. I'm sorry, but there's no way he's survived."

"I'll go out there. I'll find him."

"I'm still in charge of safety on this base, Ms Turner, and those doors are staying closed."

Gradually, the hangar emptied, leaving Lucas's mother alone.

# 10

Far away from the base, water was peppering the surface of the lake, while wind rattled the fences surrounding it. Lightning scorched the sky.

Deep under the surface, Lucas's body was still floating, held fast. He should have been long dead, but somehow he wasn't. He was breathing, drawing the oxygen-rich black fluid into his mouth with each breath. His body was extracting the oxygen from the liquid, like a baby before it's born.

Lucas's eyes were open; he was somewhere between sleeping and awake, between life and death. As the lightning flared, it lit up the lake, and Lucas began to see shapes within it. He saw his father reaching out for him. Then it wasn't his father. It was something else, something dark and black with long twisting arms. Lucas tried frantically to get away. As he turned, he saw the Terraformer pointing at him. It was powering up, gathering blue light. Lucas knew it would fire, and he tried to protect himself with his arms. The blue flame burst out of the Terraformer and danced around Lucas. With the blue light came other shapes: his house on earth; Anora, spinning in a star-filled sky; Nova base: huge, functional and sterile. Then, as the blue light faded, he saw his mother floating in the water beside him. He tried desperately to get her attention, but she flew away from him into the distance just when he was about to reach her. The shapes faded, and Lucas was alone in the blackness, the only illumination coming from the lightning. He tried to swim up but couldn't move. The lake held him fast.

The storm was getting more agitated. The wind was twisting and turning, and the rain was coming down hard, thick and fast. Then, suddenly, lightning struck the surface of the lake. The jolt of electricity caused the lake to bubble and churn.

The energy hurtled through the lake, reaching deeper and deeper until it hit Lucas and reverberated through him. He jerked and shook as he was briefly electrified. Then the electricity moved on. As it progressed, every part of the lake began to stir, and Lucas felt himself move, bubbles pushing him upwards. Within moments he had breached the surface and could feel the sharp sting of rain lashing his face.

He struggled through the thick liquid and finally made it to the shore. The black substance slid off him as he lay on his back, wallowing in the relief of being alive. Now free from the protection of the lake, Lucas began to feel the icy chill of the wind that the storm had whipped up. He was freezing, kilometres from the base and completely alone.

The lake continued to froth, both from the effect of the electricity and the rain and wind tearing at its surface. It was hard to make anything out but, just for a moment, Lucas thought he saw an arm rising out of it. Then it was gone. His imagination must have been playing tricks on him.

He took his backpack off to investigate the contents. The flares were broken and sodden, and the food had become inedible mush. He took the communicator out and shook it, listening to the water rattling around inside. He turned it on, but nothing happened. He put the backpack and its useless contents to one side. Suddenly, he remembered something and checked the side pocket. His father's medal was still there. He took it out and placed it in his overalls.

Then, in the middle of the lake, he saw it again: an arm reaching, electricity sparking around it. He stood up to get a better look. Now there was another arm and some kind of head. As the head appeared, the creature shook the black liquid off and made a terrifying sound. It was something Lucas had never heard before; a combination of an animal roar, a human scream and a powerful electric pulse – like a monster being born from rage. If Lucas hadn't already been freezing, the sound would have chilled him to the bone.

The creature was advancing through the lake towards the shore, electricity dancing over its black body. As it came closer, it became clear to Lucas that it was broadly humanoid. However, it had long, misshapen arms and crooked, twisted legs. It was also enormous – close to three metres tall – and moved with strange jerking movements. As it made its way out of the lake, it feverishly looked around, still screaming.

Suddenly, the creature stopped and turned towards Lucas. Had it seen him? He couldn't be sure, but he backed away anyway. It was out of the lake now and still moving towards him. Lucas reached the fence. There was nowhere else to go. He turned, fell to his knees and felt around for the hole. He couldn't find it. Behind him, he could hear the creature getting closer. It was still screaming, but now he could hear the crackle of the electricity that surrounded it and the fizz of the rain as it hit its electrified body. Lucas turned to face the creature. It was reaching for him, getting closer and closer. Finally, it leant in and, just centimetres from Lucas's face, opened its mouth wide and screamed.

# 11

Lucas cowered against the fence, making himself as small as possible. He closed his eyes and waited for the end to come. Then, suddenly, the screaming stopped, leaving only the sound of the wind and rain. He tentatively opened his eyes and saw nothing. The creature had gone. Maybe it had never existed. Could it have been another trick of the lake, like the things Lucas saw within it? He wasn't hanging around to find out. He frantically searched the fence, this time finding the hole that Becky had cut. He squeezed through it.

On the other side, Lucas considered his options: the communicator was broken, there was no shelter nearby, and he had no idea where the other cadets were, and no food or dry clothes. To top it all off, his breather had been lost somewhere in the lake. The situation was pretty bleak.

There was only one option. Lucas headed for the base. Every step was difficult. Sometimes the wind would push him backwards, and he would have to brace himself, so he didn't fall over. Then the wind would come at him fast from behind, causing him to stumble forward and, several times, to fall onto his knees.

Meanwhile, the rain lashed at him ferociously. He was soaked through, and his overalls clung to his body. He could barely see for the water in and around his eyes.

Every muscle ached, he had blisters on his feet, and any exposed skin was bright red from the cold, but he kept going, thinking only about making the next step and the one after that. He knew it was probably hopeless and doubtful he would make it back, but his mum was somewhere on that base, and Lucas was all she had.

Kane was wrong about survival; it wasn't just about being prepared – although Lucas would have given anything at that moment to have a fully stocked backpack – it was about a fire deep inside, a fire that kept Lucas moving despite the futility of his situation.

Suddenly, Lucas's thoughts were interrupted by a growl. He turned to look behind him and saw only rain. It must have been the wind.

He continued fighting on. There was the growl again. He turned and saw a humanoid shape a little way away, surrounded by electricity. The rain evaporated off the creature, giving it a glowing, fantastical appearance. It wasn't screaming now but grumbled and grunted as it shuffled on. It seemed to be following him. Lucas tried to quicken his pace, but the terrible conditions made it almost impossible. He turned back to check on the creature. It wasn't there. Where had it gone? Was it hiding? Was it a figment of Lucas's desperate mind?

Lucas was scared, cold, wet and struggling to breathe. The lack of oxygen had weakened him, and he stumbled on the rough terrain. He held his father's medal tightly, hoping it would give him strength. He thought he saw the creature several times: to the left of him, behind, to the right. Each time it was gone when he took a second look. Lucas was more scared when the creature wasn't there. He assumed it was pursuing him for food, the main driving force for all animals, so when it disappeared, he feared it would suddenly pounce from wherever it was hiding.

It was now almost impossible to move forward. Lucas's body ached, and his fingers were turning blue in the freezing storm. His shortness of breath meant his footsteps were getting shorter. Then he saw the base, probably no more than two kilometres away. He tried to use the lights to inspire him to move. It couldn't be long now, just one step and then another, but it didn't work this time. Lucas was desperate for oxygen and gasping for air. He was so close to the base now, but it was too late. He collapsed on the floor, and his father's medal rolled out of his hand to rest on the planet's surface just ahead of him. Lucas lay on the ground and continued to be battered by the wind and the rain, his body completely still.

# 12

At the base, Pearson was examining some circuitry in his small workshop when Lucas's mother burst in.

"You've got to help me. He isn't gone. I know he isn't."

"What are you talking about?"

"They're saying Lucas is dead, but I know he isn't. I just need to find him, but they won't let me leave the base."

Pearson thought for a moment. "I know where we can go. Come with me."

Soon, Lucas's mother was following Pearson up the ladder leading to the observation tower.

"If he's out there, we'll see him from here."

Pearson handed Lucas's mother a pair of digital binoculars. "Use these," he said.

He started walking around the platform, checking the screens on the cameras. Lucas's mother used the binoculars to search avidly through the tower windows.

"Nothing but wind and rain on the cameras," Pearson said. "Even if there were someone, we'd never see them."

"He's out there somewhere; I know it."

Meanwhile, Lucas was unconscious, face down on the ground. His father's medal lay centimetres away from his hand. He was barely breathing and what breaths he managed to take were long, and rasping. He was running out of time.

While Pearson checked the screens, Lucas's mother scanned the landscape centimetre by centimetre. She saw nothing but swirling rain.

Then came a break in the storm. Just for a moment, the clouds parted, and the two moons of Anora shone down on the planet's surface, the shafts of light visible through the still falling rain. The light hit Lucas's father's medal, resting at just the right angle in the dirt. For a second, it shone brightly before the clouds came over again.

It was enough to catch Lucas's mother's desperate eyes. "What was that?" she asked.

"What was what?"

"Section D13, a reflection, a light. I don't know what, but it was something."

She rushed with Pearson to the camera that monitored that section of the planet. Pearson adjusted the joystick, and the camera moved around, carefully examining the area.

"Look," Lucas's mother said, jabbing her finger at the camera's screen. "What's that, there?"

Pearson looked carefully at the spot Lucas's mother was indicating. He wasn't sure. "It could be someone," he said. "Equally, it could just be some rocks."

"It's enough for me. I'm going out there."

"If you just wait until the storm passes..."

"It'll be too late then. He's all alone. I'm not going to leave him there."

"Then obviously, I'm coming with you."

The two of them rushed down from the observation deck to the hangar. They opened the doors to find Kane waiting for them.

"I thought you might try something like this," he said with menace. "I'm not going to allow you to put this base at risk."

Lucas's mother replied angrily. "It's your fault my son's out there. I'm going to get him. Pearson, get the PEV ready."

Kane looked sternly at Pearson. "Don't you dare."

Pearson didn't know what to do.

"Who are you more afraid of, him or me?" Lucas's mother asked, matter-of-factly.

Pearson went to get the PEV ready.

Lucas's mother turned to Kane and said, "I'm leaving, and you can't stop me."

Kane drew his plasma rifle and pointed it at her. "You know I can," he said.

"Fine, do what you have to do."

She turned away from Kane and started walking towards the PEV.

Kane raised his rifle, "Stop," he shouted.

Lucas's mother ignored him and kept on walking.

Kane's finger moved to the trigger. He aimed the rifle directly at Lucas's mother's back. She mounted the PEV, joining Pearson in the cab. Kane, admitting defeat, lowered the gun. The hangar door opened, and the PEV was off and out.

Soon it was hurtling across the surface of the planet. It skimmed the edge of a crater, causing it to suddenly veer off course. Pearson quickly corrected.

Lucas's mother admonished him. "I thought you knew this planet like the back of your hand?"

"In the daytime, when there's no rain or hurricanes."

They could barely see through the windshield but continued to speed along.

They got to section D13.

"He should be right around here," Lucas's mother said.

"I can't see anything. Hold on, what's that?"

Something was lying on the ground. Pearson wrenched the brakes, and the PEV skidded in the wet dirt, coming to a stop centimetres from Lucas's head.

Lucas's mother rushed down the PEV's ladder. She cradled her son's head in her arms; his skin was chapped and cracked. In his delirium, he murmured something. She leant close.

"What's he saying?" Pearson asked.

"It sounds like he's saying, 'it's coming.'"

"What's coming?" Pearson asked. He looked around fearfully. Then he saw, not far away, a shape moving through the storm. No, it wasn't anything, just an illusion created by the rain.

The sky was alive with lightning again, striking the ground around them. Lucas's mother was worried. She called Pearson out of his stupor, "We've got to move."

"I know, I know. Here, give him this." Pearson handed Lucas's mother a breather, which she placed in his mouth. He was breathing, but only just.

Pearson hoisted Lucas onto his back and carried him up the ladder to the PEV. Lucas's mother picked the medal up and slipped it into her pocket.

They took off towards the base. The lightning added an extra obstacle, with Pearson having to lurch the PEV to the left and right to avoid it as it struck the ground. He spun the wheel to the left, and the PEV missed the lightning but struck a boulder, forcing it briefly onto two wheels before falling back again. Then lightning hit the ground to their left, and the PEV lurched to the right before dropping into a crater. Pearson hit the brakes hard, but it wasn't enough. It hurtled out of the other side of the crater and was launched into the air, landing badly and toppling onto one side.

"PEV's done," Pearson said. "It's not far, though. We can make it on foot.

Lucas's mother dragged Lucas out of the PEV. She and Pearson pulled him up and carried him along between them. They were only a couple of metres from the vehicle when lightning hit it, causing it to explode in a fireball behind them.

They moved as quickly as they could, fighting the wind and rain every step of the way. Pearson opened the hangar door, and they staggered inside and sat up against the wall. Lucas's mother held her son close as the hangar door closed behind them.

# 13

Lucas woke up in his room. His mother was by his bed, and his father's medal was draped on his bedside table. His mother had been crying, but she seemed angry when he woke.

"Where did you go? What did you do? I was so worried about you."

She started crying again and hugged Lucas tightly. "I couldn't lose you as well."

"It's OK, Mum, don't worry, you won't."

"But where were you?"

Lucas didn't want to get into trouble for breaking into the experiment at the lake. "It doesn't matter. I'm OK now."

"Thank God we managed to get to you."

Lucas's mother sat back and touched her son's forehead. "Looks like the fever is breaking. You should start improving now. Do you think you're ready for some visitors?"

"Visitors?"

"Your friends have been worried about you." His mother gestured towards the doorway where Williams, Peterson and Becky were standing.

"I guess so."

She beckoned them over. "Come on in. He's ready to see you now."

The three cadets entered the room. Becky was the first to speak. "Hi, Lucas, are you feeling better?"

"I am, thanks."

Williams spoke next. "We were worried about you."

Lucas's mother stood up. "Why don't I give you and your friends some time to catch up."

She heavily emphasised the word "friends" and smiled at Lucas. She was clearly glad that he had made some. Lucas felt pretty good about it too.

"Let me know if you need anything, honey," she said as she left the room.

"No problem, Mum, thanks."

Once Lucas's mother was a reasonable distance away, Peterson and Williams looked at Becky. She sighed and sat down on Lucas's bed. "Lucas, I need to explain something to you."

"What is it?"

"I am not your friend, we are not your friends, and you shouldn't start to think we are."

"I don't understand," Lucas stammered.

"You're not like us. You're weak and untrained, and you'll regret it if you tell anyone what happened out there."

There was no anger in her words. She spoke them slowly and calmly as if reading from a script.

"You can't hide from us," Williams added menacingly.

After everything he'd been through, everything he'd done, after saving Williams's life, this is what happened. He felt his stomach sink and despair grab hold of him. What was the point of trying? What was the point of anything? He felt his lip start to quiver, but he wasn't going to cry. He didn't want to give them the satisfaction of seeing that they'd broken him.

However once they had left the room, the tears came thick and fast. On his own, he didn't have to protect his mother's feelings, and he didn't have to look strong in front of the cadets. He wept freely, consumed with hopelessness and loneliness. Eventually, he cried himself to sleep.

That evening the storm came again. Lucas lay in his bed, tossing and turning. His usual nightmares about the planet and the Terraformer now included the cadets, who appeared as giants, with Lucas weak and small before them. There was also something else – a glimpse of what he had seen on the planet's surface. It was big and loud, but Lucas couldn't put his finger on what it was.

The water pounding on the roof, crashing thunder and lightning flashes conspired to wake Lucas from his troubled dreams. He lay on his bed listening to the sounds of the storm. Then he sat up and picked up his father's medal, turning it over in his hands.

"Sorry, Dad. Sorry, I can't be better, stronger; for you and Mum." He picked up the tablet. He'd never needed his father so much. He reached across time and opened the message.

*Lucas, here I am light-years from home, and my time is now very short. My greatest sadness is that I will never see you again. It is painful to think of all the things that I will not get to experience with you, all of those firsts that will define you in later life: not least your first girlfriend and, of course, your first heartbreak. I think my most significant loss is the chance to continue speaking to you and hearing your ideas and passions. Every day you become more fascinating, and more inspiring. It breaks my heart that I will not get to hear all the ways that you will change the world.*

*But despite all this, I cannot regret coming here and taking a chance, chasing the dream of a new world and a fresh start for humanity on a green planet full of possibility and hope. There comes a time in a person's life when they realise there are things greater than themselves, and that dream was more important than me. I hope one day you can understand. Care for your mother for both of us, and remember how much you are loved.*

Lucas stared at the message for a few moments before launching the tablet angrily across the room.

It crashed into the wall, and the screen shattered. Realising what he had done, he was overwhelmed by the desire to cry again. "What about me?" he said quietly to the remains of the tablet. "Why wasn't I the most important thing? If you loved me, why did you leave me?"

The plea could receive no answer. His father's last message hadn't helped at all. If anything, it had left Lucas more confused than ever.

In an effort to get a grip on his churning emotions, he got out of bed and walked to the window. He stared out into the stormy Anora night and tried to imagine his father's dream: an actual planet with trees, rivers and green rolling hills. It was difficult to see Anora as anything other than either desolate, cold and empty or ravaged by merciless storms.

Then he saw it. At first, there was nothing, and then it was only a few metres away: the creature from the lake. It had definitely seen Lucas this time and observed him before approaching as if Lucas made it nervous.

The creature was just as terrifying as before. With the screaming gone, however, and in the safety of his room, with its reinforced windows, Lucas could appreciate the creature's beauty and the bright yellow electricity that surrounded it. He was drawn to it. Lucas placed his palm flat against the glass, daring the creature to come close. For a few moments, it did nothing but look quizzically at him. Eventually, however, it sloped towards the window and placed its hand on the other side of the glass, matching Lucas's palm. Then, in the blink of an eye, it was gone. Just for a second, Lucas felt like he'd made a real friend.

# 14

After what happened on the planet's surface, classes were cancelled while an investigation took place. Kane was suspended from his teaching role and told to focus on what was now considered to be the much-needed transition of the base from military to civilian control. This left Lucas with free time to fill. His mother, still believing that Lucas had friends, was content to leave him to his own devices, assuming that he would be spending the day with the Nova cadets.

Instead, Lucas went onto the planet's surface to investigate the area outside his room for evidence of the creature. Next to the window were two marks that looked like toeless feet. The ground around the marks was scorched, presumably by the electricity that surrounded the creature. Lucas traced the footsteps away from the window. They were solid and clear for about four metres, then vanished. He crouched down to examine the last footprints. They didn't get faint or fade away, they just stopped. Where had the creature come from?

As he was considering this, some of the Nova cadets turned up, stuck for something to do without military drills to enjoy. Becky, Williams and Peterson were with them.

"Hey, geek freak, what are you doing?" Peterson taunted.

"You don't like me, you've made that clear, so can you just leave me alone?" Lucas replied from his position on the ground with the footprints.

Becky placed her hand on Peterson's arm. "He's right, he's not worth the time."

"You would try and protect your little boyfriend."

"He's not my boyfriend."

"No, more like a pet," Peterson said, turning to Lucas. "Hey, little pet, can you bark like a dog?"

"Please, leave me alone. I haven't done anything to you," Lucas pleaded.

"You don't have to do anything. Your existence is irritating. You're a coward."

Lucas leapt up, flushed with anger. "I'm not a coward." He pushed Peterson hard. Taken off guard, Peterson skidded over and fell onto the ground. The other cadets thought this was hilarious, but Peterson was enraged.

"You don't push me. You can't push me."

Lucas, calmer now, suddenly realised what he'd started. "I'm sorry, I didn't mean to hurt you. I just want to be left alone."

"You couldn't hurt me, but now you're going to feel some pain."

Lucas backed away. "I don't want to fight," he said.

"I don't care what you want," Peterson replied, sending a quick jab to Lucas's face.

Lucas didn't have the energy to raise his hands, and he didn't want to do anything that seemed aggressive. He just wanted it to be over. Peterson hit Lucas again, and this time he fell backwards.

Peterson towered over him. "Get up and fight me."

"I don't want to," Lucas implored.

"Coward," Peterson screamed with venom.

The other cadets watched, doing nothing to intervene. Friendless and broken, the tears came in floods, Lucas's body shaking as he wept. He couldn't control it. He'd tried to be brave for his mother and father, he'd tried to cope with all the difficult things that had been thrown at him, but he couldn't – it was too hard. His tears seemed only to encourage Peterson and Williams, who mocked Lucas relentlessly for crying. Some of the other teenagers joined in. Lucas looked imploringly at Becky, but she stood quietly, in solidarity with her friends.

Then everything seemed to stop. It lasted for a fraction of a second, and only Lucas seemed to notice it. Lucas felt heat gather behind him in that tiny sliver of time, like a ball of fire emerging in the air. Then there was something else, large, close, hot and breathing. Lucas turned and saw it. The creature was so near he could feel the pulse of the electricity as if it were moving through his own body. Lucas scrambled backwards to where the other cadets were standing.

There was a moment of realisation as the students looked up at the incredible sight. The creature seemed to sense their fear and rose, screaming with that horrible electrified sound. Then all hell broke loose.

No amount of military training could have prepared the cadets for what they were seeing, and, even if it had, none of them had ever been close to a combat situation. Some of them screamed, some ran, and some did both. The creature advanced towards them, swinging its long, strange arms. It caught a couple of teenagers who were frozen with fear. One of them was Peterson, unprepared for the sudden switch from bully to bullied. As he was on the floor, the swipe of the creature's arm whistled over Lucas's head, missing him completely. Instinctively, he ran over to Peterson and the other fallen cadets to check that they were OK. They were breathing but unconscious.

Unfortunately, Lucas's selflessness meant that he missed the mass run to the door. The students powered in, pulled the air clamp, and sealed it tight. They stood behind the sealed door, staring out as the creature stomped towards it. It pounded on the door causing electrical sparks to fly off it. Lucas stood up. The beast was now between him and the door. It stopped hammering the metal with its fists, turning instead to face Lucas.

# 15

The monster was no longer screaming but continued moving towards Lucas.

Lucas cried out, "Stop, "Leave me alone."

The monster stopped. Its shoulders slumped, and it looked at the ground. It seemed upset.

The cadets inside the base stared out of the door's window with a mixture of curiosity and terror. Lucas glanced towards them and then back at the creature. It remained unmoving. It didn't seem scary anymore. If anything, it seemed lonely like Lucas himself.

"Come here," he said, almost whispering. The creature shuffled forward. "Stop." It stood still. Lucas allowed himself a small smile.

Lucas slowly and carefully walked towards the creature, hands outstretched to show he meant no harm. He was still afraid, but he was also interested, and his curiosity was taking over. He moved closer until he was within touching distance. If he touched the monster, though, it was bound to be angry; to roar and lash out. It was also possible that the electrical power fizzing all over it would electrocute him. To make contact would be perilous, and yet Lucas knew he had to. He reached out and gently placed his hand on the monster's side. He could feel the power move from the creature through to him. It was warm, almost pleasant. The energy flowed through his skin and into his bones and a tingling sensation washed over him. Then, suddenly, Lucas felt a surge of power course through his brain. For a moment, probably less than a second, there was a rapid flow of information: images of the planet before they had arrived: cold, barren, peaceful; then images of machines digging into the rock and beginning to build; the base and the Terraformer dominating the sky. With the pictures was a flood of emotion: pain, loss and fear. A single tear ran down Lucas's cheek, and he took his hand off the monster. The connection was severed. The creature looked directly at Lucas. He was sure it was going to scream, to tear him apart. Instead, it did nothing but stare at him for a moment. There were two bright yellow orbs where the creature's eyes should be, and, for a second, they seemed to glow more brightly. The air around the creature shone with power, and a whirlpool of light formed. The monster's body disintegrated, consumed by the swirling energy. A moment later, there was nothing but a whisper.

Lucas was confused. He stood for a couple of minutes waiting for the creature to come back, but it didn't. Lucas turned back to the base, where the cadets inside were still transfixed by what had happened. Lucas walked up to the door and waited silently. The teenagers looked at each other, and one of them hit the door release button. Lucas walked in with a fixed, emotionless expression on his face. Out of a sense of new-found respect, or possibly fear, the cadets moved out of Lucas's way, allowing him to pass through the middle of them, which he did, silently, while they watched him in wonder.

The rest of the day on the base was chaotic. The cadets told their parents what had happened. The parents then went to either Kane or Lucas's mother in terror. Meetings took place, but Lucas's mother was insistent: there was no life on Anora. There couldn't be. The military had thoroughly surveyed the planet before and after the Terraformer had started its work and found no lifeforms. Kane was noncommittal about the creature, but he did comment that if the military were still on the base, it would be protected against any threat.

Nathan retrieved the footage from the cameras outside the West entrance. He ran it through the main screen in the command centre for Lucas's mother and Kane. The footage was fuzzy and unclear. Nathan wound it backwards and forwards. Lucas could be seen on the ground, and there was no mistaking the dancing electricity in the air.

"There's something there," Nathan said. "I don't know. It could be an electrical malfunction."

As the footage continued, Lucas could be seen walking over to the electrical shape and reaching out to it. As he touched it, the shape fizzed away to nothing.

"The boy," Kane declared, "the boy's behind this."

"Be careful, Commander," Lucas's mother said firmly. "That's my son."

"At the very least, we need to talk to him about what happened."

"I told you, I've looked everywhere. Wherever he is, he doesn't want to be found."

Nathan looked unsure but eventually said. "I think I know where he might be."

In the observation tower, Lucas stared down at the planet below. He seemed transfixed by it, lost in a deep, trance-like state. He did not turn as his mother ascended the ladder and hauled herself up to sit next to him. She had never seen him like this.

"Lucas, are you OK?"

"Why did you make us come here? I was happy at home."

"It's hard to understand, but some things are bigger than one person."

Lucas grunted at this familiar argument. His mother kept trying. "I know you were happy there, but you didn't know how bad things were. The Earth was running out of food, the water was becoming undrinkable, and the pollution in the sky was making people sicker every day. There's no future on Earth. This planet is the only hope for humanity."

Lucas's mother anxiously wanted a reaction, some indication that Lucas understood. Instead, he kept staring at the planet's surface. "It's scared," he said.

"What is?"

"This planet. We came with our machines, cutting and drilling into it, making the sky boil. We never asked for permission."

For a moment, his mother was lost for words. "I know you're finding it difficult here, and you feel scared sometimes."

Lucas turned and looked directly at his mother. "It's not just me."

Before Lucas's mother could respond, Kane's voice interrupted from the bottom of the ladder.

"Are you ready now, Ms Turner?"

Lucas's mother gently touched her son's shoulder." I'm sorry, but we've got to go. They want to talk to you."

Kane's voice could be heard again. "Bring him down, or I'll come up. It's time for the boy to explain himself."

# 16

Lucas sat in a chair in a small room with Kane and his mother. It was weird to see them standing next to each other.

His mother spoke first. "Lucas, what happened out there?"

Kane was weirdly quiet but stared directly at him. His mother walked over and put a comforting arm around his shoulders. "In your own time," she whispered.

Lucas took a deep breath. There was so much to say, but he knew none of it would be believed. Starting at the beginning, he told them about being outside and talking to the Nova cadets (missing out the specifics of the bullying, as, despite everything, he didn't want to get the cadets into trouble). He got to the moment when the creature arrived and stopped, assessing how best to describe what he'd experienced.

"It's the planet," he finally blurted out clumsily.

"What do you mean?" his mother probed.

"The planet doesn't want us here, it's..." – he struggled to find the right words – "it's in pain."

His mother looked confused. "What are you trying to say, Lucas?"

"Don't you understand? The planet sent the creature to stop the colonisation."

Kane couldn't take it anymore. "Come on, boy, there's no creature, you know that. Even your mother said it was impossible. But something did happen out there, didn't it? Something scared those cadets. Some trick you played. What did you do, boy, what did you do?"

Lucas's mother leapt to her son's defence. "Hang on a minute, Lucas hasn't done anything."

"You and your son have caused nothing but trouble since you arrived here. Another example of civilian interference in what should still be a military operation, but this is a step too far. He did something to those cadets."

"Why would he?"

"Maybe he felt embarrassed about getting lost yesterday or his failure to take on the training robot. Maybe it's just his general lack of ability."

"Shut up," Lucas screamed, anger overtaking him. "Stop talking about me."

Kane grabbed Lucas roughly and hoisted him out of his chair, pushing him against the wall. "How dare you talk to me like that. I'm in charge here. Now tell me what you did."

"I'm not scared of you," Lucas shouted back. "I don't have to be scared of you anymore."

Lucas's mother angrily grabbed hold of Kane's arm and tried to pull it off. "Let go of my son."

Lucas turned to his mother. "I don't need your help. It's all your fault. You brought me here, to this place I hate, where I'm afraid all the time. I don't need you, I don't need any of you, and I don't have to be scared anymore."

As he shouted these words, a whirlpool of energy formed behind Kane. Lucas's mother let go of Kane's arm and stood back, watching the creature develop in the air. She was scared but, like any scientist, curious too.

Lucas looked Kane directly in the eyes and said, calmly and quietly, "Let go of me."

Kane paused, unsure of what was going on. Sensing the colossal presence behind him, he released Lucas and turned around, just in time to see the creature scream and lash out with one of its long arms. The arm hit Kane and sent him flying across the room. His body clattered into the wall, and he slumped to the ground. Conscious but injured, he looked up at the creature with terror. The beast rampaged through the small room, mangling the chairs and throwing them against the walls. It turned towards Lucas's mother, raising its arms.

"Stop," Lucas said.

The creature paused and considered for a moment. Then it screamed and raised its arm to strike.

"Stop," Lucas shouted.

The monster swung its arm at Lucas's mother, and she drew back in fear, anticipating the impact.

"Stop," Lucas begged, "please."

The creature dropped its arm just in time.

Lucas's mother stared in horror at her son. Lucas could not meet her eyes.

The creature turned to the door and hit it with its arms, sending it flying off its hinges. It turned to look at Lucas. Lucas hesitated for a moment but then walked over to the monster and held its hand, feeling the powerful energy flow through him. He looked back at his mother.

Still horrified by what had happened, she pleaded, "Don't go."

"I have to," Lucas said before turning and walking off, hand in hand with the giant beast.

# 17

With Lucas and the creature now gone, Kane tried to stand. Stumbling, he touched his leg. "It's broken," he said through gritted teeth.

Lucas's mother helped him out of the room, and they struggled to the command centre. Kane glared at the shift supervisor sitting in the command chair. The man got up quickly, and Kane dropped into his seat.

"Critical personnel only. Everyone else leave," Kane commanded.

Some of the staff left. Others looked at Lucas's mother, unsure who was in charge. She assessed Kane, deciding whether to challenge him. She sighed and looked back at the staff members waiting for her response, nodding to let them know it was OK to leave. The command centre emptied except for Pearson and a few other vital personnel.

Kane tore the radio off his belt and yelled into it.

"Troops deploy. Defence strategy."

"What are you doing?" Lucas's mother asked. "There's no military contingent on the base."

"If there's no army, Ms Turner, then one must be built, which is exactly what I've been doing."

Outside the command centre, organised running and preparing could be heard. Within minutes the Nova cadets were lined up in front of

Kane, armed with plasma rifles and standing to attention.

"Nova cadets," Kane barked. "You are the last line of defence against the alien threat. It's time to make your mark on history."

"But they're too young," Lucas's mother protested.

"They are fully trained soldiers, ready to defend this base."

"But you saw what happened outside."

"Outside, they were unprepared, unorganised and unarmed."

Lucas's mother saw children dressed as soldiers in full combat suits.

"You said there were no guns on the base."

Kane gave a self-satisfied smile. "I lied."

"But your leg, you can't go down there. Who's going to lead them?"

"I'll take command from here. I'll be able to see everything that's going on and will stay in constant communication."

Kane gestured to Pearson, standing at one of the computer consoles. "Pearson, show me the creature," he instructed.

Pearson started flicking between the various cameras that monitored the base.

Lucas's mother was angry. "We don't know anything about the creature; where it came from, what it can do. We need to find out what they'll be facing before they go down there. I'm telling you to stop this now."

"I have fifteen trained soldiers at my command. How exactly are you going to stop me?"

Lucas's mother eyed the cadets again. They stood, focused and rigid, staring straight ahead. Beneath their steely eyes, however, Lucas's mother could see hesitation and nervousness. She couldn't be sure what would happen if she pushed Kane into a confrontation, what he might ask his "soldiers" to do. She decided now was not the time. She thought of her son, alone with the creature.

"What about Lucas?"

"The cadets will try to bring your son back, but their mission is to protect the base. It will be unfortunate for your son if he gets in their way," Kane finished ominously before turning away from Lucas's mother to focus on the monitors.

Pearson stopped changing cameras. The creature could now be seen in a dark tunnel, illuminating Lucas, who walked behind it. It was thrashing around, destroying drilling and maintenance bots.

Pearson indicated the screen. "It's in the maintenance tunnels."

"Then that's where the cadets need to go to take it down."

Pearson was looking at a map of the base on one of the monitors. "They'll need to penetrate at the main power conduit to shut off the maintenance and bots with the console. The creature's destroyed many of them, but quite a few are still operational, and they can move at some speed. If you don't power them down, there's a serious risk of an accident. I can talk you through it."

Kane turned his chair and addressed the cadets. "Today is the day you've been working towards. Put fear aside, rely on your training, and you will be heroes. Fear is your enemy; fear makes you weak; fear can destroy you. Do not let it. Make me proud." He caught Becky's eyes, and she smiled and nodded, acknowledging his approval. "Engage the enemy."

The cadets moved off, quick marching to the lower levels.

"This is insanity, Kane," Lucas's mother implored. "I will be contacting Earth command about this."

"By the time you get hold of them, the monster will have been destroyed, my cadets will be heroes, and I will be expecting Earth to approve the return of this base to full military control."

"Fine, then I'm going with them."

"I'm afraid I can't allow that."

"I don't care what you allow. That's my son down there."

Kane trained his gun on Lucas's mother, "You're not going anywhere and believe me, this time I'll use this if I have to."

Lucas's mother could see that Kane was serious and slumped into a chair to watch the monitors, helpless to do anything for her son.

Deep in the bowels of Nova base, Lucas sat in the darkness, looking up at the unsettling shape of the luminescent creature. They had smashed their way to the base's lowest levels and were surrounded by the wreckage of drilling bots. The maintenance bots that were still functional flew past them, clearing tunnels of debris and patching up wiring and plumbing. Despite the destruction Lucas and the monster had caused, drilling could still be heard in the distance as the remaining undamaged machines continued to carve new tunnels to expand the base.

"I heard you," Lucas finally said. "Even when I was at home on earth, I could hear you speaking to me. I could hear your pain."

The creature stood in silence, staring at Lucas with the glowing yellow orbs that stood for eyes. They were the only vaguely human attributes on an otherwise featureless face.

"Why are you still here? Why haven't you disappeared?"

The creature looked upwards. Lucas could hear movement in the levels above.

"They're coming, aren't they? Why won't they leave us alone?"

As if in acknowledgement, the creature let out a scream of rage that echoed through the tunnels. Lucas knew that it was a declaration of war.

The Nova cadets had reached the main power conduit and console. Williams hit a button, and the screen showed dozens of sub menus, which controlled every aspect of the base.

Williams spoke into his microphone. "At the console now."

Pearson came back through his earpiece. "You need to shut down maintenance and drilling in sections A7 to B13, that will power down the maintenance droids, but leave the main functions in the lower levels operational, including air and lighting."

Williams and Peterson started hitting the relevant buttons. As machinery shut down, the oppressive silence grew until the cadets could hear only their nervous breathing and the rapid beating of their hearts.

Kane's authoritative voice came over the cadet's earpieces. "Watch your flanks and stay in formation. Move steadily and slowly forwards."

Peterson opened the door that led to the main tunnel, and the cadets stepped through one by one.

They progressed a little way before stopping at a tunnel branching off to the left. The lighting inside was flickering on and off intermittently. The cadets peered down it.

"Where should we be heading now?" Williams queried into his headset.

Pearson came back. "I'm not sure. We haven't got the creature on camera at the moment. It seems to have quietened down."

Kane's voice took over. "Head to the monster's last known location. Take your time. Be ready for anything."

The cadets continued to progress slowly, trying to keep all directions covered. Soon they came to a mess of twisted metal: drilling bots bent into strange shapes by the creature. The pile of bots had been angrily jammed into the tunnel, floor to ceiling. There was no way to get by.

"We'll have to head back the way we came," Williams commanded.

The cadets turned and stopped. Lucas had stepped into the tunnel a little way ahead of them. He stood utterly still, his face emotionless. He was blocking the way back to the main power conduit and the exit out of the tunnels.

"This isn't a good idea," he said. "Leave now, or you'll get hurt."

"This doesn't have anything to do with you," Williams replied. "We're here to stop the monster. Get out of the way and let us do what we've trained for."

Lucas didn't move. "You don't understand what's going on here. You have to leave."

Peterson chirped up, his mocking voice sounding shakier than usual. "Get out of the way, nerd, or we'll move you."

Lucas spoke slowly and carefully. His voice was changing, becoming deeper. A hint of electricity danced through it. It was as if the creature and Lucas were becoming one. "You bullied me and laughed at me just because I was afraid. But being afraid isn't weak or stupid. On this planet, it's the only thing that makes sense. You're going to understand. You're going to be afraid now."

The tunnel was bathed in the dancing yellow light of the creature as it rose behind Lucas, screaming. After it had risen to stand at its full height, it remained still, its body pulsating with rage, like a vicious dog on a lead.

Lucas continued. "You think your guns will protect you. They won't. You think your guns will take away your fear. They won't. Those are real guns. Are you prepared to shoot? Are you prepared to kill? How many of you are ready to fire, and how many would rather walk away?"

No one moved. The cadets tried to stare straight ahead and remain focused on their training. However, in the cold tunnels, some of them could feel tense sweat dripping from their brows. Others were shaking. Eventually, one of the cadets at the back dropped his gun. The sound of it hitting the floor echoed through the silence. Another cadet followed, and then another. They ignored Kane's voice, which was coming loudly through their headsets.

"What are you doing? Pick your guns up, arm yourselves."

Peterson and Williams were among the last armed cadets. They looked at each other and finally let their guns fall to the ground. Only Becky was left. She was pointing her weapon directly at the creature.

Peterson pleaded with her. "Becky, don't. Just put the gun down."

"But I can kill it. I can save the station."

Williams addressed Becky as calmly as he could. "But we don't know what it will do."

Peterson's voice quivered with emotion as he said, "I don't want to die down here."

"Dad," Becky implored through her headset. "What do I do?"

Kane didn't hesitate. "Be strong, be a hero, save the base. Kill it."

Becky didn't move. Her body was rigid, her gun trained on the creature. She stared at her target, daring it to move. Responding to the challenge, the creature pounded the cabling that ran along the walls on each side of the tunnel. Electricity sparked and twisted in the air. If the display of rage was supposed to unnerve Becky into dropping her gun, it didn't work. She continued to stare without moving or blinking.

Kane's voice came through the headset again. "What are you waiting for? Kill it."

Lucas watched Becky and the creature. Since his "interrogation", his brain had been a fog of fear and rage, with destruction always at the centre. As he watched the standoff, however, the fog began to clear. He could see at that moment the potential consequences if they continued their trail of destruction: the base collapsing, people running in terror, cadets lying on the ground, their bodies broken. Lucas knew he had to stop the monster. He stood between it and Becky. He tried to talk as calmly as he could while walking slowly towards the creature. "Stop, please stop, don't hurt them." Lucas's plea had no effect. The beast lurched towards the cadets so quickly it became a blur of yellow electrical power. It ran into Lucas without slowing, sending him flying backwards to land – unconscious – at the cadets' feet. That's when Becky started to fire.

# 18

There was an electrical junction box on the left tunnel wall, about twenty metres ahead of Becky. She swung her gun around in one quick movement and hit it with a burst of plasma, causing it to explode in a shower of sparks. The lights went out, and for a moment, there was chaos. Some of the cadets screamed as they were plunged into darkness. Illuminated by the electricity dancing over them, all they could see were the flailing arms of the creature.

Becky shouted, "Infrared." The cadets suddenly understood her plan, each pressing the button on the side of their helmets. Their visors dropped down in infrared mode, allowing them to see in the dark.

Kane's voice was coming through loudly in Becky's ears. "Is it dead? What happened to the lights?" Becky responded by taking off her headset and letting it hang loosely around her neck.

The creature, unsettled by the sudden darkness, backed away from the cadets as it tried to understand what was happening. It was bent over, with its head touching the ceiling. Its arms continued to swing wildly. There was no way past it. Becky could not be sure how long it would take for the monster's eyes to adjust to the darkness. She searched frantically for an exit. The nearest door was still behind the creature. She shot the cables running along the walls next to it. Sparks fired briefly into the air. The beast screamed and backed away. She fired again, and the monster retreated further. It passed the door. This was their moment.

"Corridor on the left, fifty metres," Becky shouted to the other cadets. They ran towards the door.

Kane, Nathan, and Lucas's mother watched the monitors in the command centre. There was little to see except the bright, blurry mess of yellow that was the creature. They could hear the cadets running and screaming.

"You've got to bring them back up," Lucas's mother shouted.

"They'll be fine. They've just got to remember their training."

Realising she wasn't going to get through to Kane, Lucas's mother approached Nathan quietly. "This is crazy. He's going to get those kids hurt, or worse."

"I agree," Nathan whispered. "But what can we do?"

"We need to learn more about the creature. Where it came from, how to stop it and how it's connected to Lucas. Will you help me?"

Nathan nodded.

"Good, follow me."

With Kane still focused on the monitors, Nathan and Lucas's mother slipped quietly away.

The creature continued to rage blindly in the tunnels, its arms crashing into the floor and walls. The cadets ran past it as quickly as possible, piling through the door. Becky looked at Lucas, who was on the floor and starting to regain consciousness. She crouched down and helped him sit up. "We've got to go," she said.

This seemed to give Lucas a burst of energy. He was suddenly aware of his situation. Without infra-red, all could see was the creature still raging. He shouted at it, "Please stop this. You've got to stop." Any power he'd had over the monster now appeared to be gone. All his words did was help it locate its targets. As it looked towards the source of the noise, Becky thought it seemed to be picking them out in the dark. Its eyes were adjusting. She grabbed Lucas and dragged him up. "We've got to go. Now!"

Lucas kept staring at the creature as Becky dragged him towards the door. "Something's different," he said.

"I don't care about that. I just want to get out of here."

Lucas wasn't afraid. Just like his mother, curiosity was taking over. "I just don't know what it is."

The creature moved towards them.

As Becky pushed Lucas through the door, it swung at her. She dropped just in time, the creature's arm sailing through the air above her head. She rolled into the corridor, leapt up and hit the switch. The door slid shut just as the creature's arm collided with it. For the moment, the cadets were safe.

Lucas was deep in thought. Finally, he turned to the cadets. "I know what's different about the creature," he said, "it's getting bigger."

# 19

Nathan and Lucas's mother were sitting in Nathan's workshop, looking at a screen.

Lucas's mother was reasoning. "Lucas must have seen the creature before he was outside with the cadets. Do you remember what he said when we found him on the surface?"

"Yes," Nathan replied. He said, 'It's coming.'"

"He was talking about that thing. He must have seen it when he was lost. Is there any way you can find out where he went?"

Nathan started tapping at the keyboard. "The central database should contain the data from the cadet's trackers." He pointed at a red dot on a map, surrounded by blue ones. "Here's the data from the day of the expedition. Lucas is in red, and the other cadets are in blue."

Nathan hit a button, and the tiny dots went into fast forward. A timer showed the day advancing as the dots raced around the map. Suddenly, the red dot disappeared, and Nathan hit pause.

"This was when his tracker stopped transmitting, but we haven't got anything significant mapped for that area. It's weird."

Lucas's mother gasped. "I know what's there." She picked up the keyboard and started typing. "If I override your authority, I'll be able to bring up the cameras for that section."

"But that area won't have any cameras..." Nathan trailed off when he saw a series of extra cameras listed under Lucas's mother's ID. She clicked on one of them, revealing the fenced off lake.

Nathan looked at the screen, amazed. "Your experiment."

She started winding the footage forward. They watched the staff leaving and the cadets breaking in. Then Lucas fell into the liquid. Lucas's mother touched the screen. "You poor thing," she said as they watched him struggle out of the lake again. Then they saw the creature pulling itself out of the black liquid and following Lucas.

Lucas's mother leant back in her chair, a look of horror on her face. "It's all my fault," she said.

In the tunnels, the door began to buckle under the relentless pounding of the creature on the other side.

Becky was talking to Lucas. "How can it be getting bigger?"

"I don't know," Lucas replied. "But it definitely is. Earlier, it was around three metres tall, approximately the same height as these tunnels. When we escaped just now, it was crouching to get around. It has to be at least a metre taller."

"It doesn't make any sense."

"So, until now, the big electricity monster made perfect sense?"

Becky allowed herself a small smile. "Fair enough," she replied.

Williams interrupted them. "I don't think that door's going to last long."

Peterson, panicked and angry, pushed Lucas hard. "It's his fault," he said, on the verge of tears. "It's all his fault. We should have left him to the creature."

"I'm sorry," Lucas said. "I'm so sorry."

"Maybe sorry isn't good enough," Peterson shouted, pushing Lucas again.

Becky grabbed Peterson. "I don't know what's going on exactly, where that thing came from, but I suspect we're all to blame."

Williams stepped forward. "But he spoke like that monster. Like it controlled him."

Becky eyed Lucas suspiciously, pointing her gun at him. "He's right. Why were you talking like the creature?"

"I don't know. Honestly, I don't. It's as if I could feel its pain, its anger, but I can't feel anything anymore." Lucas seemed strangely sad about it.

Becky lowered her gun. "Everyone, leave Lucas alone for now. Peterson, you find us a way out of here."

"But I thought Williams was in command."

Becky gave Peterson a stern look. Instead of confronting her again, Peterson looked sheepishly at his digital map. He scanned it and turned it in different directions but came up with the same answer from every angle.

"Oh no, we're in trouble, we're in so much trouble."

"Why?" Becky asked.

Peterson showed her the map. "This tunnel isn't finished, so it doesn't go anywhere. It's a dead end, and the only way out is back past that thing."

The cadets all turned to look at the thick iron door, which was buckling under the ferocious blows of the creature.

Lucas grabbed Peterson's map.

"What's this?" he asked, showing Peterson a square icon on the map positioned in the tunnel behind them.

"That's just another maintenance console," Peterson replied. "I don't see how that helps."

"Can we override the main console from here?"

Peterson looked at Lucas, confused. "Yes, I think so. Why?"

" I can get us out," Lucas said.

# 20

Nathan and Lucas's mother burst into the command centre.

"Where have you been?" Kane demanded.

Lucas's mother ignored him. "We know where the creature came from, and it isn't from this planet."

"Are you saying we brought it from Earth?"

Nathan pitched in. "No. We made it. Or at least Lucas did."

Kane, whose attention had been on the darkened monitors, turned his chair and stared directly at Lucas's mother. "What's he talking about?"

"The last time we tried to transform a planet, it didn't work. My husband was supervising the transformation. Everything seemed to be going to plan. The atmosphere was changing, and storms were starting, like on Anora. But the surface wasn't developing at the same rate. In fact, it didn't seem to be changing at all. They thought the Terraformer wasn't working hard enough. They kept tweaking it. They pushed it far beyond its design specifications. Eventually, cracks started to appear."

She paused, almost overcome by the emotion of that day. A moment later, she continued. "They got as many people off the planet as they could before the Terraformer exploded. When it went, everyone left on the base was lost, including my husband, and the planet became a useless, polluted rock."

"I've read the reports, Ms Turner, and I'm aware of what happened," Kane said impatiently. "But I don't see how it's relevant here."

Lucas's mother continued. "They'd got it wrong. To redesign a planet requires more than just the Terraformer. The Terraformer changes the atmosphere, pumps nutrients into the air, and creates clouds and water, but there's something it can't do. It can't create lifeforms."

"And why would we want to create lifeforms, Ms Turner? Surely that would be incredibly dangerous."

"I'm talking about tiny microbial lifeforms: bacteria, fungi, algae, that sort of thing. Without microbial lifeforms, the ground can't be broken up into soil – plants can't grow or decay. Without these microscopic creatures, there can be no grass, no crops, no life on Anora at all. That's why we set up the lake. A pool of protein-rich amniotic fluid in which microbes could grow, stimulated by electricity and DNA replicators."

Kane was angry now. "You set up an experiment on my planet without my knowledge?"

Lucas's mother was exasperated. "It isn't your planet, Commander Kane. Earth command knew about the experiment, but they felt it would make people nervous, so they kept it on a need-to-know basis. Something went wrong. Your cadets went there, Lucas fell in, and that creature came out."

Kane looked at Lucas's mother in horror.


The cadets were lined up in the tunnel, ready to go through the door. The pounding continued. One of the hinges had come off, and the other was nearing its breaking point.

Peterson clutched his tablet, swiftly tapping buttons. He addressed Lucas with some venom. "This had better work, nerd."

"If it doesn't, what are you going to do? We'll all have been smashed to pieces by a walking lightning storm."

Peterson smiled; he always appreciated a good comeback. He shouted to Becky at the front of the line. "Ready to go."

The bolt that held the final hinge in place snapped.

"Now, Peterson," Becky commanded. "Do it now."

Peterson hit a button. A few hundred metres away, a machine could be heard spinning into life.

"It will take a few seconds to get here," Lucas said.

"I hope we've got a few seconds," Becky replied.

As if in response, the door fell to the floor. The creature saw the cadets and screamed. With nowhere to go, all the cadets could do was cower away from it. It reached in for them. Surely this was it.

Suddenly, one of the maintenance bots struck the creature, carrying it away from the door and clearing the path to the exit.

"Go, go, go," Becky commanded. "If Lucas is right, we haven't got much time."

"Fifteen seconds," Lucas reminded her.

Lucas's idea was to use the maintenance bot to take out the creature, allowing the cadets to escape before the machine rotated again. Unfortunately, the bot in their section was on a short, fast track, giving them only fifteen seconds to get out before it hit them. Lucas had done the maths in his head. If running, the fifteen cadets should be able to get through the door with 2.5 seconds to spare.

The cadets hurtled down the corridor towards the exit. Lucas counted in his head as they ran. "One, two, three, four, five..." They were nearly halfway to the door; they would be fine. "Six, seven, eight, nine..." The door was only a few strides away now. They were at the section where the cadets had discarded their weapons. Lucas trod on one, slipped and rolled over. Becky paused to help him, but Lucas waved her on. No point in her getting hurt too. "Ten, eleven, twelve..." Lucas was back on his feet, but his ankle hurt. He limped as quickly as he could. The other cadets were through the door, their hands reaching to him. "Thirteen, fourteen..." Lucas could hear the bot approaching. Just a few more steps. Lucas fell. The bot was bearing down on him. Williams grabbed him and hauled him through the door as the bot sped past, missing him by a few centimetres. The cadets relaxed for a moment and caught their breath.

The creature was back up now and advancing towards the cadets. The bot sped into it, but this time the monster was ready. It grabbed the bot, twisted it into a mess of metal, discarded it and kept moving. Williams hit the door switch, and the cadets ran for their lives. They didn't stop until they reached the command centre.

# 21

Lucas's mother grabbed Lucas in a vice-like hug as soon he entered the command centre. At the same time, Becky and her father shared a firm handshake.

Deep in the bowels of the base, loud banging and crashing noises could be heard. The sound was moving upwards, getting closer.

"It's coming," Lucas told his mother. "I thought I could control it, but I think it was controlling me."

"That's what fear does," she replied. She held him close. "I'm so sorry," she said. "After your father died, I was so afraid I wouldn't be able to carry on and take our work forward. I felt like I had to come here and face my fear, but I didn't think about you and how you would feel. And now this creature... it's all my fault."

"It's not your fault. It's the planet," Lucas protested. "The planet's afraid. It sent the creature to stop the drilling, the terraforming."

"I'm sorry, Lucas, the creature didn't come from the planet. You created it when you fell into the experiment at the lake."

Lucas backed away from his mother in horror. "No, I didn't. I can't have done."

"You fell into an experiment designed to create life. When the lightning struck the water, it activated, and the lifeform it created was based on you. It did the best it could - that's why the creature is humanoid. As well as your human characteristics, it also took the fear you keep buried inside you and turned it into rage and destruction."

"No, that's not right," Lucas protested. "The planet's been talking to me for months, even when I was on Earth."

"I think that was your fear, even then. It doesn't matter what Kane says, it's OK to be afraid, but you've got to accept that fear and understand it. If you bury it, you can end up controlled by it."

"So, what do we do now?" Lucas implored.

The noise from the tunnels below was getting louder and closer.

"I don't know, Lucas, I just don't know."

Suddenly, the floor shook, causing everyone in the room to stumble. Pearson ran to the corridor, which seemed to be the centre of the impact. A bump was forming in the floor, which continued to shake. Each time it did so, the dent grew until it wasn't a dent at all but a huge hole. Some people ran, but some stood and watched the hole form in shock. The creature reached through with its long arms and hauled its gigantic body out of the tunnels. The people who had gathered ran and screamed as it stomped towards them. The monster had to be six metres tall now, but it was still growing, more quickly now than before. It turned Pearson's way and began moving towards the command centre. Pearson ran back inside. "It's heading this way," he shouted. "And it's really growing in size."

The fearful screams of the people in the corridor were getting louder as the monster approached.

"That's it!" Lucas's mother said, thinking out loud. "Lucas's fear created it, and now it's feeding on fear. The fear of the cadets in the tunnels, the fear of the people in the base. That's why it's growing."

"It's getting angrier too," Pearson cried as the monster exploded into the command centre. It was visibly increasing in size now, and the centre could barely contain its enormous bulk.

Kane trained his gun on the creature from his chair and began firing. Bolt after bolt of plasma pounded into it with no effect. The creature didn't even seem to notice the bolts striking it. Within a minute, Kane had emptied his gun and could only drop it to the floor and stare up at the monster helplessly. As cadets and staff dashed out of its way, it crashed through the room, tearing through monitors and consoles as if they were made of paper.

"What are we supposed to do?" Kane shouted. "How do we stop it?"

"I don't know," Lucas's mother responded. "At first, it was connected to Lucas. It wasn't fully alive, only forming when he was afraid. Now it's independent – an entirely new life form."

Pearson watched the screens as the monster crashed around. "If we don't do something soon, we're in real trouble. It's destroying key systems. Without air and water, we'll die on this planet."

"I think it might be worse than that," Lucas said as he watched the creature.

"How can it be worse?" asked Pearson.

"There's one thing that I've always been more afraid of than anything else. Something I've hated for years, that's haunted my dreams every night. I think the creature feels the same way."

"Oh no," Lucas's mother gasped as she realised what Lucas was talking about.

As if in acknowledgement, the creature punched the command centre wall that led to the surface, crashing through it easily. Air poured out of the base, and the cold, harsh atmosphere of the planet started rushing in. Lightning was forming in the sky as the evening's storms began. The monster lumbered out of the command centre, one target clearly on its mind.

"It will destroy the Terraformer," Lucas's mother exclaimed. "If it succeeds, all life on this planet will be wiped out."

# 22

"I've got to go," Lucas declared. "I started this; I've got to stop it."

"But there's nothing you can do," Lucas's mother implored. "It isn't connected to you anymore."

"I think maybe I can still get through to it. I've got to try."

Lucas's mother grasped his arm. "Then I'm coming with you."

Lucas gently removed her hand. "No, you've got to stay here. Try and get these computers working and shut the Terraformer down. Only you can do that. I've been afraid for so long. I've got to be brave now."

Becky walked over. "I'll go with him," she said.

Lucas hugged his mother. She held him tight, reluctant to let go. They both knew that this might be the last time they would ever see each other.

Becky walked over to her father and grasped his hands. "I know you find it difficult to say how you feel, but you've always tried to do the best for me."

Sitting there, facing imminent destruction, and seeing his daughter for possibly the last time, even then, the words wouldn't come for Kane. "Remember your training," was all he could think to say.

Becky couldn't help but smile at this typical lack of emotion. She turned and left the base with Lucas.

Lucas's mother looked around her: sparks were flying out of computer consoles, lights were flashing, alarms were blaring, and small fires burned around the room. "Pearson," she shouted, "gather together any technical personnel you can. Let's see what we can get working. Kane, get the medical staff moving through the base to help the wounded. We're also going to need to do something about these fires. Maybe your cadets can help with that. Let's get to work."

Outside the base, Becky and Lucas pursued the creature. It had a significant head start, but they could just make it out in the distance, shuffling towards the Terraformer.

The storm was starting to take shape, and the rain was getting heavier. They jogged in an attempt to get to the creature before it reached its destination.

"What are we going to do when we reach that thing?" Becky asked.

"I don't know," Lucas confessed. "Find some way to get through to it, I guess."

"And if we can't?"

"We're just going to have to find a way."

They jogged in silence for a few minutes.

"Lucas," Becky said finally. "I'm sorry for the way we treated you."

"It's OK."

"No, it isn't OK. It's just that after mum left, dad didn't know what to do with me. He tried to get people to look after me: aunts, uncles, babysitters, but I misbehaved, scared them all off. Finally, he had no choice but to take me with him wherever he was stationed. I worked so hard. I learned about discipline and the military way of life, devoting every waking hour to it. Do you know why?"

They stopped jogging, and Lucas gave Becky his full attention, understanding that she had probably never shared these feelings with anyone before. "No," he said. "No, I don't."

"It was because I was scared. I didn't want him to leave like mum did. I thought if I could become the best soldier I could, he'd keep me around. I suppose I'm saying that we all have things we're afraid of. Because of my fear, I couldn't see anything outside of the military. I couldn't see you. I became a bully, and I'm sorry."

Lucas smiled at Becky and this genuine insight into her heart. "It's OK; it really is," he said.

Becky smiled back and then found herself suddenly embarrassed. She jogged on ahead, shouting back, "Hurry up, we've got an Armageddon to get to."

Lucas smiled at this too and jogged after her. At least if he was going to get blown up, it would be with a friend.

Soon they reached the creature, but, unfortunately, it had already made it to the Terraformer. The familiar blue fire billowing from it lit up the evening sky. The storm was in full flow now, and the rain was coming down hard. Lucas and Becky looked up at the massive monster as it began to hit the Terraformer with its fists.

Lucas shouted up at it. "Stop this. You've got to stop." The wind drowned him out. He found rocks and threw them up at the creature, but they disintegrated as they collided with its body.

"What do we do now?" Becky shouted.

Lucas looked at the Terraformer. At the very top, right within the creature's eye line, was a viewing platform. It could be reached by a ladder that ran up the side of the structure. It had to be a thirty-metre climb.

"We go up," Lucas replied.

Lucas mounted the ladder first, with Becky following. As they climbed, they could feel the impact of the creature's blows against the Terraformer's side. The Terraformer was the most reinforced structure on the base, but there was only so much punishment that even it could take.

The ladder was wet, and the climb was difficult, with rain and wind lashing at them. Angry that he had not destroyed the Terraformer already, the creature pulled its fist back and hit it with one mighty blow. The structure shook as if struck by an earthquake, and Lucas lost his grip. He began to tumble, colliding with Becky, who grabbed him with one hand, the other hand just about managing to retain its grip. Lucas struggled back onto the ladder, and they carried on climbing. However, the blow from the creature had done serious damage to the Terraformer. As they got to the platform, Lucas saw that a long crack had already formed in the machine's body, with smaller ones branching off it. Blue light was spilling from them. It was like all of the nightmares that had possessed Lucas since his father's death. It seemed there was now no way of stopping the Terraformer from exploding.

# 23

Lucas and Becky reached the platform and clambered onto it. Lucas put himself right in front of the creature's face and yelled, trying to be heard over the wind and lightning. "Hey, remember me?"

The creature did not appear to remember him, or at least it gave no indication that it did, choosing instead to continue hitting the Terraformer. Bits of masonry tumbled down from above them. Lucas picked up a chunk of concrete and gave it to Becky. "Try and get yourself noticed," he said.

"What if we make it angrier?"

"To be honest, any reaction would be a good thing right now."

Back at the command centre, the rain pouring in through the hole in the dome had, thankfully, put out most of the fires. Lucas's mother commanded a team of technicians who worked on the consoles and monitors. "Looks like we've got a partial connection, Pearson. How does it look to you?"

Pearson looked at his screen excitedly, "That's it, I think you've got it. Readings are coming online now."

He watched the figures and charts come into colourful life on his screen.

"Any chance of performing a shutdown?" Lucas's mother shouted.

Pearson's face dropped as he digested the data. "I'm sorry, but there's no chance at all. In fact, it's quite a lot worse than that."

Kane was concerned. "What do you mean?"

Lucas's mother came over and looked at the data on Pearson's screen. She grabbed his keyboard and rapidly hit the keys, bringing up different charts and graphs. The conclusions were the same. "He's right. The Terraformer's taken too much damage. It could explode at any second."

Lucas's mother stepped back from the screen, feeling the pressure of the situation push down on her. There was nothing she could do. It was all going to end on a planet far away from earth, as it had for her husband. She looked around the command centre and felt what it must have been like for him. She stared at the screen and wondered what he would have done with his last few seconds. Then, suddenly, it came to her, like a voice from the past.

"Vent the secondary air processor," she said.

Pearson did as he was told and looked back at the screen.

"Good job," he cried, "you bought us another few minutes."

"You can change the world in a few minutes," she said, almost to herself.

"What?" asked Pearson, confused.

"Nothing," she replied. "Just something my husband used to say."

Lucas and Becky continued throwing debris at the creature, to no effect. Then Becky got lucky and hit one of the yellow orbs that served as its eyes. It howled in pain and swung one of its arms at her. She jumped back just before the arm hit. They had the monster's attention now.

Lucas shouted at it. "You've got to stop now. This isn't the way. People will die." The creature threw open its mouth and screamed. If Lucas hadn't known better, he would have thought it was laughing. Lucas reached out to touch the beast, but it moved away from him and went back to hitting the machine. More blue fire was spilling out now, and the structure felt unstable.

"What now?" Becky shouted.

"I've got to get the connection back," Lucas replied. "I know it's there, it's faint, but I can feel it." He looked down at the thirty-metre drop. "There's only one thing I can think of."

The platform's safety railings were pretty mangled, and it was easy for Lucas to find a space where they had broken off altogether. He looked down at the ground far beneath him. He was terrified. He couldn't do it. Then he looked over at the base. It looked tiny against the backdrop of the vast, empty planet: a little offshoot of humanity, building a new life in the stars. Suddenly, he realised what his father's email meant. Some dreams were bigger than any one person because they had to be. No single person could do it by themselves. They each had to play a part: from his mother and father, who had designed the means of humanity's salvation, to the engineers who had built the Terraformer. Even Kane had a role to play. Now it was time for Lucas to play his part too. He looked at Becky. "Sorry," he said before leaning away from the platform and letting himself fall. Becky gasped as she watched him hurtle towards the ground.

As Lucas fell, he wondered if this was it. Would he be killed, like his father, on an alien world at the mercy of the Terraformer, or would the monster he had created remember their connection and reach out and save him? While plummeting, he watched the rain falling towards him and felt the pull of gravity and the bracing chill of the air. He could hear the creature still pounding the Terraformer. His plan hadn't worked. He had been falling for long enough now; the planet's rocky surface couldn't be far away. He closed his eyes and accepted his fate.

Then suddenly, he was swung violently away from the ground. He opened his eyes to find that the creature had him in its hand. Lucas held on tightly with both his arms. He could feel the connection with the beast re-establish itself, the rush of information flooding his brain. There wasn't long. The creature was sure to drop him any second, severing the tie again. He tried to focus his thoughts on something peaceful to drive the fear from his mind. It was difficult; life had been so challenging since his dad had died. Then he found it.

His mind went to a summer's day back on Earth. His father had strung an old tyre from a steel lighting unit behind their housing block. He'd told Lucas it was like the swing he'd had in his garden as a child. Lucas remembered his father showing him how to swing on the old tyre. He felt the summer breeze on his face and the gentle, rocking motion of the swing, but, most of all, he felt his father's love, warm and true.

The creature set him on the ground and looked at him. The storm continued to rage in the sky, and the Terraformer still shook with the violent build-up of energy, but the creature was calm. It picked Becky up from the platform and set her down next to Lucas.

"I think he understands now," Lucas said to Becky.

Becky looked up at the Terraformer. It was cracked, broken and pulsating with energy. "It's too late now, though, isn't it?"

"Yes, I think so."

Lucas touched the creature gently, feeling its warm energy for the last time.

The creature walked over to the Terraformer, staring at it as the energy built to a loud pitch. It moved forward and wrapped its long arms around the machine, covering the network of cracks with its body. If it was trying to stop the Terraformer from exploding, it failed. A few moments later, the Terraformer blew up.

# 24

Becky and Lucas scrambled across the wet, stony ground, managing to find a large piece of metal to shelter under. They watched as the Terraformer exploded into the creature. For a moment, it looked like its body might be able to contain the blast, but within seconds the energy was pouring out of it in a steady stream.

The energy was now bright green. It flowed over everything, and all that it touched glowed and changed. The stream was so powerful that it reached way beyond the base, hitting the lake, which roiled at its touch. Then it moved further still, weaving its way over the whole planet, touching mountains and valleys, bringing transformation everywhere. Eventually, the energy finished its journey, coming full circle to hit the creature again. It held its arms in the air to allow the remaining power to flow into the sky. The storm clouds parted, and the wind stopped.

Lucas came out from behind the metal shelter and looked up at the creature. It fell to its knees, exhausted and in agony, its breathing shallow and strained. It looked back at Lucas and stretched its arms out to him. Lucas ran towards it, reaching out to touch it. Before he could get there, it gave a last cry of pain before evaporating away to nothing for the final time.

Becky walked to Lucas and held his hand. They stood on the lush green grass, looking up at the bright blue sky. They felt the sun warm their faces as they took large gulps of clean, fresh air. It was a beautiful day.

When Becky and Lucas got back to the base, people were already coming out to look in wonder at their surroundings. When Lucas saw his mother, he ran over and put his arms around her. "Look what we did, Mum."

She looked around, trying to take everything in. She was lost for words for a while until finally settling on, "It's incredible." Lucas explained to his mother what had happened. She surmised that when the energy from the Terraformer had been filtered through the creature's body, it had become something new. Teeming with life, it transformed the planet at a rate no one could ever have dreamed of. There was no doubt that the creature had given its life to protect Becky and Lucas, but had it known that it would also be giving them paradise?

People were nervous about the new world at first, believing it to be an illusion that would fade with time. Gradually, however, their confidence increased, and teams were sent to explore and chart the planet. They found snow-capped mountains and rivers, fields, fruit and vegetables. The experiment was now just an ordinary lake, with bright, cool water. The machinery around it was broken and covered in flowers.

As weeks passed, Lucas began to explore on expeditions with groups of friends. Discovering new caves or forests. Often, he and Becky would take trips by themselves, holding hands and watching the sunset, comfortable and happy in each other's company.

People built houses out of stone and metal reclaimed from the destroyed Terraformer. Lucas's mother was offered the governorship of the new colony and an array of spectacular homes. She took simply what she had promised Lucas, a small house with a garden, shed and garage. Eventually, Lucas, and the planet's other inhabitants, stopped calling the world Anora or its technical, numerical classification and just referred to it as home.

**If you enjoyed this book, please consider posting an Amazon review. You'll help other readers find these exciting adventures and encourage me to write more!**

# A preview of the next exciting Tomorrows book...

# 1

The plant was vast and beautiful, its thick tendrils dancing together as it curled away into the distance. Large, bright fruits grew from the vines in abundance, adding blue and red dashes that perfectly complemented the deep green leaves. Every so often, the plant would shoot sudden bursts of pink pollen into the air that would drift lazily to the ground. Anyone who saw it would surely be in awe of it.

For the girl, it was a day like any other. She floated along the length of the plant, using its vines to propel her, gently brushing its leaves. With the lightest touch, she felt the texture under her skin, experience telling her if a leaf was dead or alive. She would gently twist off the dead ones to allow new shoots to grow. Where the plant had become tangled, she would untwist the vines; where it had become dry and brittle, she would moisten it. The plant gave her the greatest reward for her efforts: it allowed her to consume its wondrous fruit. The fruit was sweet and supplied all the nourishment she needed.

She was always working to help the plant grow and thrive. With her aid, it would spread its love to all.

The girl existed only to serve the plant. It was all there was and all there had ever been. Sometimes, she would stop her work and wonder at its vastness. The plant seemed to approve of her appreciation, its vines surrounding and caressing her. She would close her eyes and hold the warm, soft leaves to her skin.

Occasionally, she would pull herself along the plant as quickly as possible, seeking its end. She was always comforted that there was no end; there was only the plant protecting her in a great, never-ending loop. Afterwards, she would feel foolish that she had challenged its omnipotence.

When she was tired, she would stop and push herself deep into the plant, and it would wrap itself around her and pull her close. She would sleep, knowing she was safe and protected. When she woke, she would continue her work.

Sometimes she would encounter the other "not-plants." She wouldn't seek them out, but they were pleasant enough company. They would talk about the plant, its beauty and their love for it. It was nice to meet others who loved the plant as she did. They would rarely stop for long; they were keen to get back to their service.

Every day was the same, but she was content. What more could there be to life? Then things changed.

The sound was faint but unmistakably wrong. The rhythmic, electronic noise couldn't possibly come from the plant; therefore, it could not exist. Unfortunately, the muffled, repetitive thud did not go away. It was strangely familiar as if she had heard it before, in another life. But there had been no time before the plant, so she ignored it. However, it worked its way into her mind, unsettling her, undermining everything she knew to be true. Eventually, she had no choice; she had to find out what it was.

She moved slowly along the length of the plant, listening intently. Sometimes the noise grew louder, sometimes quieter. Gradually she narrowed the sound down to a section about a metre long. There seemed to be nothing significant about this part of the plant; it was as perfect as the rest. The girl couldn't see anything capable of making the strange sound. She tried to pull the plant's leaves apart, looking for a hidden device, but as she moved vines, others would twist into place to stop her. Eventually, with no other choice available, she wriggled into the leaves and branches. She suddenly realised that the plant could stop her, kill her even, by twisting its powerful vines around her. Who could blame it: her search was the ultimate blasphemy. It may have been her imagination, but she felt a hesitancy about the plant as if it was reluctant to do something that drastic. Not yet. That didn't mean it was easy to make progress; she had to fight to move, a centimetre at a time. She knew what she was doing was wrong, but with each hard-won centimetre, the sound got louder, so she continued.

The sound could only be centimetres away, but she could go no further; something flat, impenetrable, and distinctly un-plantlike was in her way. She pounded the hard, shiny surface with her fist. It made a low, clanging noise. She felt that she had seen this substance before, that it had a name. As she tried to remember what the material was called, the sound stopped. She lay still for several minutes, willing the sound to come back, craving answers. There was only silence. For as long as she could remember, the peace of her world had provided her with solace. Now, the quietness felt empty. Then the hard, shiny substance began to recede into the distance. The plant had tired of her excursion and gradually eased her out of its branches. She did not have the energy to fight, so she pulled herself backwards, helping the plant expel her. She floated in the air, exhausted. Her eyes fluttered for a moment before closing.

She could not be sure how long she slept, but she awoke suddenly to the loudest noise she had ever heard. The electronic sound was all around her now, and it was deafening. Her head was swimming, struggling to focus. As she spun in the air, her hands over her ears, something came towards her, breathing loudly: a not-plant unlike any she had seen before. It did not float like the other not-plants but moved across the floor, balancing on its two legs, each foot stepping deliberately, one after the other. It had two arms, much like herself and the other not-plants, but it was covered with something white and baggy, making its limbs and body look like they had been pumped up to twice their size. The head was even stranger: white, hard, shiny and larger than any head she had ever seen. Where there should have been a face, there was a dark semi-transparent material. If she squinted, she could make out something like a face inside the head. Suddenly a word popped into the girl's mind that seemed to describe the creature perfectly: astronaut. Then the astronaut spoke, in a hard, amplified voice, "we haven't got much time. You have to come with me. It's going to destroy everything."

The astronaut reached out to her. The girl stared at its hand, fear and uncertainty etched on her face. She turned to the plant for support, but it was limp. It must have been the noise. She grabbed its lifeless leaves.

"What have you done?" she screamed, "you've killed it. YOU'VE KILLED IT! All it wanted was to love you."

She spun around and threw herself at the astronaut, pounding it with her fists. It grabbed the girl but struggled to hold her. In a panicked voice, it said, "There's no time; you have to come with me." The girl was sobbing and fighting to break free. "No, leave me alone," she looked at the pathetic plant, "leave us alone."

The astronaut pushed the girl hard. She flew backwards, grabbing the limp leaves of the plant to steady herself. The astronaut came to a decision. "Fine", it sighed.

The astronaut's visor slid up, and the girl saw a face that meant everything to her. The astronaut reached out again, "Ayana, you've got to come with me. Please."

Ayana. It was a name she knew so well, had heard a million times. Could it be? Yes, it was her name. How could she have forgotten?

This time, Ayana took the astronaut's hand. The astronaut led her past the plant, which was beginning to stir. Although it had little of its usual strength, it still lashed and grabbed at them. The astronaut turned and punched deep into the plant. With a whooshing sound, an opening appeared. The astronaut pushed Ayana through and then followed her, the opening closing behind them. Ayana looked feverishly around, her brain overloaded with input: spacesuits, cables, flashing lights. Nothing here made any sense. She clutched her knees. Her breathing was quick and shallow. Ayana wanted the plant again: its love, its warmth. Then she stopped, seeing something that put her breakdown on hold. She grabbed the rail that ran around the room and slowly pulled herself towards the strangest thing she had ever seen. On the other side of a small round window, giant, green and blue, was the planet Earth. She turned to look at the astronaut, tears running down her face. The astronaut removed its helmet, reached out and touched Ayana's face, gently wiping away a tear.

Finally, the astronaut spoke again. "This is going to take some explaining."

To be continued in...

**TOMORROWS**
**BY DANIEL CULL**

## Space Seeds

...available now.

Printed in Great Britain
by Amazon

81131122R00078